COWBOY

ROYAL DEVILS GEORGIA

ERIN TREJO

Created with Vellum

CONTENTS

Chapter One

Cowboy

"What the fuck is that?" Mav asks as I drop the large bundle onto the couch.

"I need you to babysit," I tell him.

"Babysit? Why? What are you doin'?"

"I've got a date." I can tell by the look on his face that Mav doesn't believe that shit.

"You don't date."

"I do now. It's more of a pussy date."

"You're dumpin' this shit on my couch so you can go get some pussy?" he asks me, his voice serious. Well, of course, I am.

"I can't really take it with me."

"A body, Cowboy. It's a goddamn body!"

"Well, no shit. You think I'm gonna get pussy if I have a damn body in the car?"

"You can't leave it here," he shoots back.

"Just couple hours, brother. Then I'll get rid of it."

"Hey, Rina! Looks like we're babysittin' tonight," he calls out to his old lady.

"Whose baby?" she squeals as she walks into the room and takes in the bag on her couch. "That is a body. Not a baby."

"Not too much of a difference, yeah?" I ask with a grin on my face.

"It's way different, asshole. Why is there a body in my house?" Rina asks, crossing her arms over her chest.

"He needs a babysitter so he can get laid," Maverick chimes in.

"You're not leaving that here."

"Why not? Just a couple of hours. I don't have time to deal with it right now."

"Yes, you do. Cancel your pussy date," Mav suggests.

"Come on. You can't do a brother like that."

"Whose body is it anyway?"

"That's a long story. One I don't have time to tell you right now. Can you just watch it?"

"Watch it? You want me to watch a dead body?" Mav asks.

"Yeah, basically."

"Get rid of it," Rina chimes in. I sigh and run my hand over my face before glancing over at her.

"Please. I fuckin' said please."

"We are not babysitting your dead body, Cowboy!"

"It won't be no trouble," I snicker.

"Not the point. It's on my couch. That's disgusting in itself."

"I can put it in the kitchen if that makes you feel better."

"What would make me feel better is you getting it out of my house. Why did you even let him drag that in here?" she asks Mav as he sits next to the dead body that's rolled up in bags. He tosses his arm around it and smiles.

"He just walked in with it. What was I supposed to do?"

"Uh, tell him to get out!"

"Not that simple with a man like me. I don't take orders," I add.

"Who is it?"

"Long story. We established that already. So can he stay?"

"This ain't no sleepover, Cowboy! You get your ass back here and get the dead guy off my couch in less than two hours. It doesn't take that long to fuck."

"You're leaving it here to get some ass?" Rina's voice is filled with disbelief.

"It's more like a date," I tell her.

"A date? You don't date."

"I do now. What is it with you two tellin' me I don't date? I do date. Or I do now anyway."

"You're going on a date? Like an actual date where you don't get any pussy?"

"Yeah, somethin' like that."

"Bullshit. I call bullshit right now, Cowboy. So where the hell are you goin'?" Mav asks, not believing me at all.

"That hurts, brother. You think I can't go out with a woman and not fuck her on the first date?"

"You're goddamn right; that's what I think. I've seen you with every fuckin' club whore from here to New York, and you're tellin' me you are goin' out with some bitch and not gettin' your dick wet?"

"That's exactly what I'm sayin'." Both of them burst into laughter. I should slap the shit out of them, but I don't. That wouldn't be right, considering they are going to babysit for me.

"Have you lost your goddamn mind?" Mav asks me.

"No. Not that I know of. Since when is it a crime to take a girl out the right way? Maybe I'm not lookin' for just sex this time, Maverick. Maybe I'm lookin' for somethin' more."

"By takin' out a club whore?" Rina asks, clearly confused.

"She isn't a club whore."

"What is she then?" Mav asks with a smirk on his face. Asshole.

"She's a woman. She isn't into the club shit and doesn't know about the club," I explain.

"So you're hidin' your true identity from her?"

"I'm not hidin' shit. I'm easin' her into it. I don't even know if I like her all that much. There's no sense in draggin' her to the clubhouse if I don't like her."

"So you're taking her on a date?" Rina asks.

"Isn't that what I've been sayin' this whole time? You two are some stubborn ass fuckers."

"I've just never known you to date, brother. Always take it, fuck it, leave it."

"Well, she's different. I don't want to take her, fuck her, and walk away."

"Fine. I'll take care of this," Mav nods toward his new friend sitting on the couch.

"Yeah?" I ask hopefully.

"Yeah, I got it. Does it matter where I dispose of it?" I shake my head.

"Nope. Don't make no difference to me."

"You're gonna owe me for this shit. I wasn't plannin' on movin' any dead bodies tonight. Tyrant know about this?"

"No. And he doesn't need to either. This was personal," I tell him. It was, in a sense.

"Okay. I got it. Get the fuck out of here and go on your damn date then."

"Thanks, brother. I'll owe you one."

"You're gonna owe more than one for this shit. A goddamn date, Cowboy?"

"What if it's all worth it in the end?"

"What if it's not?" Rina asks, ruining my moment.

"You always such a downer?"

"Not usually. Enjoy your date."

Chapter Two

Annabell

"Last time I trusted you, we ended up in the back of a cop car," I tell Ruby, my best friend, as she tries to get me to go out with her.

"That's not fair! We didn't even go to jail that night."

"We were in the back of a cop car," I remind her once more.

"I know, but that was different. This is my brother's place."

"He's probably home anyway," I try and talk myself out of going with her, but she's stubborn and isn't going to let me do that.

"Annabell, don't make me beg," she whines, putting on the most pathetic attempt of a puppy dog face.

"You're not going to beg. You already know I'll go. Even if I wanted to say no, you wouldn't let me." Her eyes light up as she claps her hands and stands from her seat.

"Let's go then before he drinks all the good shit," she grabs my hands and pulls me from the couch. I groan, acting as if I don't want to go when in reality, I do. It beats sitting around the house on a Saturday night doing nothing. Ruby and I aren't with the in-crowd at college. We don't conform to their standards which leaves us off the lists to all the good parties. It's a little sad, in a way.

"You know you're going to have fun with me."

"I love you, Ruby, but your fun is dangerous," I tell her with a laugh.

"Is not. Besides, it's my brother's place. How much trouble could we get into there?" She has a point. I haven't seen Ryan in almost five years. Which is weird considering me and Ruby do almost everything together, yet she's still close with her brother.

"I don't know how pissed Ryan is going to be at us breaking and entering into his house."

"He won't care. He loves me." She grabs her keys before grabbing my hand and dragging me toward the door. I shouldn't be doing this, but what else is there to do? And besides, it's her brother. I doubt he'll mind much.

We walk out to the car and climb in as Ruby revs the engine. Then we take off down the road.

"Is he going to be there?"

"I doubt it. He always has some kind of club shit going on," she replies. I remember him joining a club a long time ago, so no one really sees much of him. But, according to him, he's always busy with club business.

"What's that like? The club stuff?"

"I don't know. He hasn't invited me to any of it. I think it's rude if you ask me. I should be allowed to come to the parties, but Ryan says they are always full of half-naked girls and booze. He doesn't want me around that."

"Really? That's what their parties are like?" I ask.

"That's what he says. I don't know how true that is. But, as I said, I've never got an invite."

"And you've never wanted to crash one of those like you do everyone else's parties?" I tease her. I can't help it. I love the girl.

"I've thought about it. I know Ryan would lose his shit if we showed up, and he didn't know. He said the guys would look at us as fresh meat, and they wouldn't hesitate to jump on us."

"I don't know. I think he's exaggerating, so we don't want to go. Maybe he's embarrassed by us."

Ruby snorts a laugh before nodding her head.

"What if you're right? What if big brother is embarrassed by us? Maybe that's what he's afraid of," she adds.

"Probably right. Or maybe he is telling the truth. Maybe those parties are downright nasty. We've never been anywhere near a motorcycle club," I tell her.

"Maybe we should find one and go check it out. I heard Ryan say that some of them are open to the public on weekends."

"Did we just make plans for next weekend?" I ask in a teasing tone. Ruby laughs, keeping her eyes on the road.

"I think we did. Now let's go drink big brother's booze." She whips the car into a driveway I never saw coming and pulls up to the house. It isn't big or fancy, but it is nice.

"This is his?" I ask her.

"Yeah, his bike is here. Wonder if he's home," Ruby answers, climbing out of the car. I'm right behind her, walking up the steps. Then I watch her pull her kit from her pocket and pick the lock. Yes, the girl knows how to pick locks, and I think it's awesome as fuck.

"Oh, look. It's open." She walks in, and I follow, not hearing anything. I assume Ryan isn't home, but then the sounds reach my ears.

"Oh my God, he's fucking someone!" I whisper scream at her. Her eyes widen, but she doesn't make a move to leave as I do. Instead, she grabs my hand and drags me into the kitchen, where she rummages through the cabinets.

"Are you kidding me?" I hiss at her. She shrugs and continues with her mission of finding liquor when I hear a deep voice behind us.

"What the fuck is this?" Ruby and I both turn at the same time to see Ryan standing there in nothing but a pair of boxers. Damn, has he grown up. I don't remember him looking this fucking good. I let my gaze travel over him before meeting his eyes. A strange look crosses his face before he looks at his sister.

"Hey, big bro! Didn't know you'd be here."

"It's my house, smartass," he retorts.

"I thought you would be out with the club. What's the new girl like?" she asks, making him smirk.

"You'd like to know. Get out of here, you little shit."

"We're not leaving. We don't have any booze, and we're broke. Deal with it," Ruby says before grabbing a bottle of Jack from the counter and twisting the cap off. I watch her bring it to her lips before taking a long pull and passing it to me.

"Fine. Stay, but I'm not done."

"No one cares, Ryan," she grumbles before grabbing another bottle of god only knows what this time. He turns on his heel, ignoring us and heading back to his room while Ruby and I grab a snack and plop down on his couch. It's not ten minutes later when he comes out with some girl attached to his arm. She doesn't look like something he'd go for. She's … clean cut.

"Thought you were busy?" Ruby asks, making me snort a laugh.

"I can't fuck with my little sister in the livin' room. Thanks for that, by the way."

"That brings a whole new meaning to quickie," I blurt out. Ruby laughs, Ryan cuts his eyes at me, and his date rolls hers. I watch as Ryan walks her to the door, apologizing the whole way. It's almost amusing to watch. Then he presses a kiss on her cheek and holds the door while she walks out.

"You two are somethin' else," he says, locking the door and coming to drop down on the couch next to Ruby.

"We're your something else. You miss us?"

"I saw you yesterday, but you, Bell, I haven't seen you in years. You've grown up." I nod my head taking another drink, feeling awkward as fuck right now. I can't seem to get rid of this tingly sensation I feel when he's this close. It must be the liquor kicking in.

"Why are you here drinkin' all my shit?" he asks, leaning back against the couch.

"We ran out, and there was nothing to do. We aren't popular, so we don't get invited to the good parties," I mumble under my breath.

"Why aren't you invited?"

"We aren't popular, I just told you. We're … oh my god, Ruby, we're dorks." A burst of laughter explodes out of her before she leans forward, resting her elbows on her knees.

"We are not dorks. We just don't get invited to parties, is all."

"Well, that's a load of bullshit. Why the hell wouldn't they want you two there?" Ryan asks, looking at Ruby. She shrugs her shoulders, so he turns his attention to me. When his eyes meet mine, I feel like all the air has been sucked from the room. I grab the bottle and take another long pull. If I'm going to make it through the night at his house with him, I'm going to need some liquid courage.

"I don't know. We're just never invited."

"Can we come to a club party?" Ruby chimes in.

"Hell no. They'd eat you two alive."

"Oh, come on. We're not that bad," I huff.

"Didn't say you were. You're exactly the type the guys would go for."

"What type is that?" I ask, needing to hear him say it. If he calls us dorks, I'm done.

"The cute little college girls. The pretty little innocent kind," he explains, causing Ruby to shoot her drink out of her nose.

"Are you shitting me right now? The little innocent kind?" she laughs loudly, and I can't help but laugh along with her.

"What's so damn funny?"

"We're far from innocent." Ruby stands and announces that she has to pee before walking down the hallway. That's when Ryan turns to me and looks me up and down.

"You're not innocent?" I shake my head as he inches his way closer to me.

"Is that right?" I nod, not able to form words right now. He's too close. Too in my space.

"We do things," I tell him.

"What kind of things?"

"Bad things." I let those words linger as he gazes into my eyes. Then he shocks me as he leans in closer, his lips nearly touching mine. We're a breath apart.

"You're gonna stop doin' bad things, Bell."

Chapter Three

Cowboy

I should have made them leave, but I couldn't. Now I'm shoving my feet into my boots with two drunk girls passed out on my couch. If the guys saw this shit, they'd get a kick out of it for sure.

I pull my cut on before grabbing all my shit and stuffing it in my pockets. I need to be at church in an hour. Running my hand through my hair, I head out into the living room to see the two of them still passed out on the couch. I walk over and grab the blanket and drape it over the two of them as they sleep. Just as I'm about to turn and walk out of the room, I hear Bell moan in her sleep. The sound goes straight to my cock. I adjust that fucker as I glance over at her. Her lips are parted, her eyes closed. She's grown up, that's for sure. She isn't the same little girl I once knew.

Shaking my head, I walk to the kitchen and grab a cup of coffee before heading out to my bike. The girls will make themselves at home just like Ruby always does.

I climb on my bike, pulling my helmet on as I do. Then I rev the engine and pull out of the driveway heading down the road.

It doesn't take me long to get to the clubhouse, and that's part of why I like living where I do. It's quick to get here when I need to.

I pull up and park, climbing off my bike before heading inside.

"Hey," Shade greets me as I walk in, smelling the eggs and bacon cooking.

"We gettin' breakfast?" He nods his head as I high-five his ass. It's always nice when one of the girls decides to cook around here. We pay them when they do extra like cooking for our no good asses.

"You look happy today," Tyrant adds when I walk over and sit next to him at the bar.

"I'm happy every day. What the fuck are you talkin' about?"

"You're too happy."

"Had a good night, brother, till my sister and her friend showed up. They both drank all my liquor and passed out on my couch."

"At least no one threw up on your shit."

"Your sister threw up on your shit?" I ask Shade.

"Yeah. She was younger, though. Didn't know how to hold her liquor. She can now!"

"Heard that. Nah, they were good. They drink a lot, so I wasn't too worried about it."

"Why don't you ever bring your sister around here? I've never seen her."

"Because you horny fuckers would be all over her, that's why."

"Oh, come on. We aren't that bad," Shade shoots back, making me grin.

"You are that bad."

"Hey, fuckers," I look over just as Maverick walks in.

"Look at you lookin' all rested and shit," I tell him with a grin.

"No thanks to you. Asshole."

"Come on. It was well deserved." Shade doesn't pay us any attention before he turns and walks away. I watch him go before turning back to Mav.

"You get that handled?"

"Yeah, it's all good. You owe me, asshole. Rina was on my ass all night," he adds.

"She was not. She probably liked that shit," I argue. She has missed her old missions at times, and it makes me wonder just how long she can go without doing something.

"Like hell. She was pissed I had to leave the house. You gonna tell me exactly what that was about?"

"Personal shit. Let's just say he isn't gonna be missed at all." Maverick nods his head, grabbing one of the coffees that have been set on the bar for us. I grab the other and bring it to my lips. I've got to have something to wake my ass up.

"Did Tyrant say what this is about?" I ask Mav. He just shakes his head. I didn't figure Ty would give up anything. That man holds his cards close even when it's club business.

"Didn't say shit to me," Mav says. I nod once as the other guys slowly trickle into the clubhouse before we all sit down and eat breakfast. The girls did a good job today. Bacon, eggs, sausage, and biscuits. You name it; they made it. I smile my thanks as they walk around the room, setting more plates of food out. The guys devour it in seconds.

"When you bitches are done eatin', we need to have church." Finally, Tyrant decides to speak. We all finish up and move from the table into the chapel, where we take our seats.

"Glad you fuckers could all make it," Ty starts as he looks around the table.

"You miss us?" I ask, making him grin.

"Not in the slightest. Let's begin. There's been talk around that some clubs are runnin' girls. Nothin' local yet that I've heard of."

"By runnin', you mean traffickin'?" I ask.

"That's exactly what I mean. As I said, I haven't heard of anything local, but I know a few girls have gone missin' around here. I can't say it's the same people responsible because I don't know. I want your eyes and ears out there. I want to know if anyone hears of anything comin' this way."

"We have family in the area," Shade chimes in.

"I know that, which is why we're here. Keep an extra close eye on your family members and the girls from the club. We don't know who they target or why. As I said, I don't fuckin' know much about this, but it concerns me enough to bring to the table. No one runs humans through here. This is our turf. We run guns. We make good money from it. That's it. Women are not on the radar and never will be. You hear somethin' I want to know as soon as you know."

"We have no idea what clubs to look out for?" Shade asks.

"No, we don't. If anyone sees someone we aren't friendly with, that's a sign. We know no one we're in bed with would do this. That's why I'm askin' you to keep your eyes open." He looks around the table as we all agree. I pull out a cigarette and light it up, blowing smoke into the air.

"Anything else we need to discuss?" Ty asks, looking around the table. No one raises their hand or adds anything else. "Then we're finished here."

The guys all stand and leave the room as I finish my cigarette. I snuff out the rest in the ashtray before shoving out of my chair and heading back into the main room.

"You okay?" I ask Shade when I see him pacing the room.

"My sister goes to school here."

"So does mine, brother. Our girls are gonna be fine," I tell him.

"What if they target one of them? College girls?"

"That'd be stupid then. They know the girls go to school. The school would know they were missin' and call that in. They have a lot of friends and shit too, brother. Let's not get ahead of ourselves," I reassure him, placing a hand on his shoulder.

"Yeah, you're right. I just worry about her out there by herself."

"She isn't by herself. She has friends, yeah?"

"Yeah, she does. And she checks in every day."

"Then don't worry until you see somethin' is different, brother. I think Ty just wants us to keep an eye out. Nothin' bad is happenin' with our girls." The more I say it, the more I question it. Maybe I should get some kind of security on Ruby. Maybe she shouldn't be out drinking and shit like she usually does.

"You rethinkin' it now too?" Shade asks.

"No."

"Yeah, the fuck you are," he snaps at me.

"Nah, my sister is good. She's always with a friend. She doesn't travel alone."

"Well, let's hope that shit doesn't come around here then."

"Heard that." I walk across the room to where Tyrant is sitting and drop into the chair next to him.

"You freaked Shade out."

"He should be freaked out. We don't have any intel. Doesn't that freak you out?" I shrug.

"Been in that position before. It always worked itself out, yeah?"

"You're right, but this is different. This is human fuckin' traffickin' brother. This is a large-scale setup, and we don't know who is behind it. That alone sets me on edge."

"Heard that. My sister and her friend go to college here. So does Shade's."

"Which is why I brought this to church. I want you guys to be extra cautious, and if you hear anything get back to me. If the girls even hear a rumor and they come to you with it, I want it. We'll check into everything we can."

"Sounds good, Prez." He nods his head before grabbing a beer. It's too damn early in the morning for me to be drinking, so I stick to my coffee.

Chapter Four

Annabell

"What are you wearing this weekend?" Ruby asks as she rummages through my closet.

"I don't know. What are we doing?" Ruby slowly turns to face me and rolls her eyes.

"The motorcycle club? Do you remember anything?"

"I didn't think we agreed on that."

"We did agree on that. And we're going to see what all the hype is about. If I hear Clarissa talk about it one more time, I'll lose my shit. She's a skank, so I know what she's doing there."

"That's where you heard it? And you're counting her as a reliable source?" I ask, unsure how I feel about that. Clarissa is a skank, and we all know it. She makes up stories to make herself look good and seem popular.

"She has been around," Ruby laughs before turning serious again. "She knows all the hot spots. I heard her talking about it the other day in the commons. She even told Virginia how to get there."

"So you overheard the address, and we're just going to show up?" I ask, needing clarification.

"Exactly. Now, what are you wearing so I don't take your outfit."

"Jeans and shirt. Take whatever you want. I want to be able to run if I have to."

"Run straight into some hot guy's bed," she adds.

"Is that all you think about?" Not that I can say anything, I've been thinking about Ryan since the other night.

"Yes, that's all my little one-tracked mind thinks about. Maybe, just maybe, we won't be the campus dorks with them." I sigh because I know she's right. I'm not even sure what deemed us the campus dorks, but we sure as hell don't get invited to anything. If you ask me, it's a little shitty, but we show up to whatever parties are happening anyway.

"Yeah, you're right. What was that?" I ask when I hear something outside.

"Probably the drunks in Three B."

"It sounded closer," I stand and head toward the hallway. That's when I hear it again. Another noise that sounds like someone is jiggling our window. I rush back into the room, slamming the door before grabbing Ruby.

"Someone's trying to break in!" I squeal. She grabs her phone before screaming that she's calling the cops. I watch her dial and tell them what's happening before hanging up and dialing again.

"Someone's trying to break in. What do I do?" I don't know who she called, but I look at the door, praying no one comes through it. My nerves are rattled, my hands shaking. I listen to the one-sided conversation for a long time before I see her move into the closet. When she comes back out with a gun, I nearly die.

"Where'd that come from?"

"It's my brothers. He left me two of them. One in here and one in my room." She holds the gun aiming at the door.

"In my closet?"

"I knew you'd say no. I hid it."

"Oh my god, I could have blown my head off," I shriek as she holds her hands steady.

"But you didn't."

"I could have!"

"Yeah, but you didn't. Now calm down and stand behind me."

I hear the rumble of bikes before I hear the sirens in the distance. In a matter of minutes, our door is opened, and Ryan walks in with his gun in hand.

"Put it away before the cops get here," he orders Ruby. I watch her move to put it away. Adrenaline slowly leaves my body, and I begin to tremble and shake. Ryan walks over and pulls me into his arms.

"Hey, it's okay. You're okay."

"She's freaked out," Ruby tells him, although I think he made that assessment already.

"I know she is. It's okay, Bell." He uses the nickname he gave me when I was younger. Tears spring to my eyes before slowly falling down my cheeks. Ryan keeps me held tightly against him until the cops get here. Then he lets me go so he can tell them what happened.

They take our statements and check the area, but they don't find anything.

"It was probably some drunk kid," Ruby announces as Ryan paces the room. He has something to say, but it looks like he doesn't know how to say it. I wish he would so he could stop the pacing shit. It's making me nervous all over again.

"Or it wasn't," he finally speaks.

"I'm sure it was. Three B is always drunk, and the idiot forgets where he lives. Once he tried the door too, and I had to direct him home," she tells her brother, who keeps eyeing me for some reason.

"You agree with her?" he asks, looking directly at me. I don't know what to say, so I just nod my head.

"I'm sure she's right. They do that from time to time."

"You're scared," he adds. Well, no shit, I'm scared. First, someone tries to break in, and then Ruby has a gun.

"Why does she have a gun?"

"Do you know how to shoot, Bell?" Ryan asks, ignoring my question altogether.

"No."

"You're gonna learn. Both of you are gonna take self-defense courses too. Hell, I'll teach you myself."

"First of all, I don't like sweating, which is why I don't exercise. I'm not getting all sweaty with my brother," Ruby tells him as she makes a sandwich for herself. I don't know how she's so calm about all of this when I'm still a shaking mess.

"Why does Ruby have a gun?" I repeat.

"Protection." Just one word from Ryan. That's it.

"I'm not comfortable with it being in my closet," I tell them.

"So put it in the nightstand. Or under your mattress," he responds, eyeing me now.

"Are you serious? If I don't want it in the closet, I surely don't want it under my mattress. You want me to blow off my tit in my sleep?" Ryan cracks a smile that nearly melts my insides. Fuck why is he so cute?

"You won't. I sleep with mine under my pillow, and I'm still here."

"You do what?" I squeal as he grins at me.

"Go pack a bag. You can stay at my house tonight," he says, looking at Ruby. I know he's talking to both of us, though. He wouldn't leave one here without the other.

"I'm not going anywhere. The cops said it was probably some drunk kid, and I believe him. They are everywhere over here," she replies calmly.

"I didn't ask. I said, pack a bag."

"What are you going to do, Cowboy? Tell mom and dad I didn't follow your orders?" she asks, rolling her eyes.

"I mean it, Ruby."

"So do I. I'm not going. We're fine. Aren't we fine, Bell?" I shrug my shoulders because I have no idea what I feel at the moment.

"She isn't fine."

"You're right; she's gorgeous!"

"Really, Ruby?" he asks, sounding exasperated by all this.

"Really, Ryan?"

"Fine. You don't want to come to my place; then I'm crashin' here tonight." Ruby looks past Ryan to the other two guys who have been standing there silent this whole time.

"Don't you need your clubmate? Tell him you need him," she says, talking directly to them. They both stand there with smirks on their faces as they watch the showdown.

"I'm Maverick," one steps forward, offering his hand to Ruby, then me. "That's Shade."

"That's hot," Ruby chimes in.

"Ruby!" Ryan snaps at her. Shade chuckles before slapping a hand on Ryan's shoulder.

"She can't help it, Cowboy. Look at me." I snort a laugh this time that causes Ruby to laugh.

"Fine, you can stay, but so can he," Ruby gives in, eyeing Shade up and down.

"He ain't stayin'. I'll see you guys at the clubhouse tomorrow." The guys nod their heads and turn to leave, leaving Ryan standing here.

"You don't have to stay. We'll be fine." I can't believe the words fell from my lips as shaken as I am, but it's true. We'll be fine. Ruby has a damn gun.

"I have good aim," she adds around her mouthful of sandwich.

"Go to bed, both of you."

"No, I'm eating."

"Take it with you, Ruby. I'm tired as fuck tonight." Ruby mumbles something I can't make out under her breath before stalking toward her room. I walk through the kitchen before I turn around, feeling his eyes on me.

"Thanks for staying." He nods once and drops onto the couch as I turn and head to my room.

"You want to sleep with me tonight?" Ruby asks as I walk down the hallway.

"No, I'll be fine. Thanks, though."

"See you in the morning."

Chapter Five

Cowboy

Sleep doesn't come. Not with visions of her in my mind. I shouldn't be thinking about her like that, but fuck, I can't help myself. The girl has grown up since the last time I've seen her. She was just sixteen back then. A kid. Now she's all grown up and filled out. I couldn't help but notice the curves of her ass.

I grab my cock and stroke that fucker, not caring whose house I'm in. She has me worked up and not in a nice way. I wanted to bend her over and pull her little shorts down her legs and fuck her over the counter. The thought had occurred to me more than once. I groan when I hear the faucet turn on.

Glancing over, I see it's her and not Ruby in the kitchen and decide to make a move. I know I shouldn't, but I can play with her a little. I rise from the couch and walk over, pressing my hard cock against her back when she startles.

"You feel that?"

"What are you doing?"

"I'm lettin' you feel how hard you make me. You feel that, Bell? All that from those little shorts you had on. I bet my brother's walked out of here with hard as fuck cocks too. You're a little tease, aren't you?" I whisper against her ear. She trembles when I slip my arm around her waist, pulling her back against me. I grind my cock against her, groaning as it begs for release.

"Turn around." She does without hesitation, and when I see the red staining her cheeks, I almost lose it. I pull my cock free from my jeans and stroke it harder in front of her. Her eyes widen when she realizes what I'm doing.

"Take it," I tell her. She shakes her head. I reach for her hand, and she doesn't pull away. She wants this, she just doesn't want to admit it, and that's okay with me.

When I have her hand, I wrap it around my cock, keeping my hand over hers. I squeeze and tug with her hand until I feel my balls pull up tight.

"I'm gonna come all over you," I warn her. I few more jerks, and I come all over the front of her. She doesn't move; she just stands there, shocked by what just happened. I let her hand go and run mine through the mess I made before bringing it to her lips.

"I-I …"

"Say no, Bell. Tell me, no." Bell opens her mouth, but the only thing that happens is me slipping my cum covered fingers between her lips. Bell closes her lips around me and sucks like she's taking me in, causing me to growl low in my throat. I knew it was a bad idea to stay here, but I wanted to make sure they were okay. I wanted to make sure whoever it was didn't come back.

I pull my fingers free before nodding toward the hallway, my way of telling her to go to bed. She doesn't move, though, just stands there unsure what to do. I wrap my fingers around her throat and squeeze lightly.

"You should go clean up and go to bed, Bell. Don't make me do somethin' else I'll regret later."

She nods her head, not a single word falling from her lips before I release her and let her walk away. My cock doesn't agree with that, but I know in the back of my mind I've already gone too far with her. She's my sister's best friend. She isn't mine to touch, to taste, no matter how much I want to.

"Fuck me," I grumble under my breath before fixing my jeans and heading back to the couch. I drop down and pull my phone out, checking my messages before I lay down and try to sleep.

When I wake up again, the sun is beating down on me through the window. I groan and roll to my side, almost falling off the couch when I hear Ruby.

"Morning!"

"Why are you so happy?"

"Why are you so cranky?" she asks in response.

"It's too goddamn early to be awake," I tell her.

"It's eleven, and I'm hungry."

"Fuck me," I grumble, running my hand over my face. I didn't realize I slept that late. I'm usually not one to sleep later than eight.

"I'll pass, but you can take us to eat lunch," Ruby says, eyeing me.

"Fine. I'll feed you, but then I have to go."

"You sleep good out here?"

"Wasn't bad. I might need to hit your couch up again," I tease her. Ruby smiles as she walks over and drops down next to me.

"It was nice knowing you were out here. Thanks for staying, Ryan."

"Not a big deal. I'm just glad the assholes didn't come back. We should get a security system put in, though."

"If you want. I don't think we need it."

"I agree with Ryan. Security system it is," I look over when I hear Bell speak. She's dressed in a pair of jeans that hug her ass and a t-shirt that shows off her tits. I groan a little and shake my head, remembering what I did last night.

"Stop checking out my friend, Ryan. You have club whores for that," Ruby chimes in.

"Fuck off, Ruby. You want to eat or not?" I ask her.

"Of course I do. Let's go." She shoves off the couch and grabs her cell and keys before looping her arm through Bell's and pulling her toward the door. I follow her, lighting a cigarette before walking out and blowing smoke into the air.

"Smoking is gross," Ruby reminds me like she always has.

"No shit. You shouldn't do it."

"I mean it, Ryan. You want lung cancer?"

"I'm fine, Ruby. Thanks for caring," I tell her before leaning down and kissing the top of her head.

"You two are so cute together," Bell chimes in now.

"That's disgusting," Ruby adds.

"I meant brother and sister, you sicko."

"Still gross. Ryan is far uglier than I am."

"Really? We look damn near like twins, Ruby," I defend myself against my sister's attack.

"We do not!"

"Like hell, we don't, sis. Just get used to it. If I'm hot, then so are you."

"That makes my stomach sick. Please stop."

"Get in your car and shut up," I finally tell her with a giant smile on my face. This girl is too much.

29

Chapter Six

Annabell

"Are you checking him out again?" Ruby half whispers in my ear as I stare at Ryan.

"No, I'm trying to figure out how the hell he can eat so much," I lie. I'm checking him out. I don't give a shit how much he eats or why.

"He's always been like a goddamn Hoover vacuum. It's weird."

"He doesn't gain weight," I add as I watch him devour more food.

"You do realize I'm sittin' here, right?" Ryan finally chimes in and stops chewing as he looks up at the two of us across the table.

"Oh, we know you're here," I murmur as I watch him take another bite.

"Do you have to watch me eat?"

"It's just amazing how much food you can consume," Ruby teases as she watches him now too. I almost laugh, but I don't.

"I'm hungry. I didn't eat last night since I was dealin' with you two," he adds. I nod my head agreeing with him but still stunned.

"So we nickname him Hoover." I shrug as Ruby barks out a laugh.

"I have a name, and it sure as hell isn't Hoover."

"Yeah, Cowboy. We get it." Ruby rolls her eyes, but I keep watching Ryan until he focuses his gaze on me. Then he runs his tongue along his finger, licking up any syrup he may have missed. The way his tongue moves is holding me hostage. I can picture him licking me, sucking me.

I shift in my seat and try to stop staring, but he knows what he did. He knows he's gotten under my skin.

"You're disgusting. Do you have to make everything sexual?" Ruby asks him.

"I'm a man eatin' breakfast. I'm sorry if you two are lost in a sexual world."

"We aren't lost!" I protest, but Ryan just raises an eyebrow at me. Okay, maybe I am a little lost in what he was doing, but to be fair, he started that mess last night.

"Right," he mumbles before finishing his food. I watch him wipe his mouth when his phone pings. He slides it out and checks it before pulling a wad of cash from his pocket and tossing it onto the table.

"I gotta go. Club shit."

"Leaving so soon?" Ruby teases.

"Club shit. I'll stop by later," he says, causing my insides to tumble. They always seem to do that when Ryan is around.

"Fine. Just go. Leave us all alone," Ruby whines as I giggle.

"I think you'll be fine. See ya," he shoves out of his seat and walks out of the restaurant.

"That was weird."

"What was?" Ruby asks.

"Your brother just up and leaving. Does the club run his life? They say come, he runs?"

"For the most part. I don't get all the inner workings, but when they call, he goes. I told you we're going to figure this club shit out when we hit that party."

"You think it's that easy? We just show up?"

"Why not? If Virginia's showing up, then we can too. Hell, we can say she invited us," Ruby adds.

"That might piss them off."

"So? They'll be pissed at her, not us. We need all the help we can get at this point, Bell." I know she's right. I know we need to find a crowd to belong to, but I don't know about just showing up to a motorcycle club uninvited.

"Are you overthinking it?" Ruby asks.

"Of course I am! Your brother doesn't let you into his club, and here we are going to another one? Doesn't that make you a little nervous?"

"My brother doesn't want us fucking any of his friends. That's the conclusion I've come to. He keeps us away, so we don't flirt," she says, making me smile.

"As if they'd want us."

"Hey, they might. Ryan isn't bad looking, and I look just like him!"

"You have a point. Maybe that's why he keeps us away. We should crash one of theirs one time and see if he loses his shit," I tell Ruby, watching her eyes as they brighten. Oh, that was a joke, and she clearly didn't take it as that. I see the wheels spinning in her pretty blue eyes.

"It was a joke, Ruby."

"But a good one. We could totally get into his club. Ryan would shit himself, but those two didn't seem so bad last night."

"No, they were pretty nice. Maybe it wouldn't be so bad." I shrug. I don't know anything about their lifestyle or what the hell Ryan does there.

"Anyway, this club is supposed to be really rockin'."

"Rockin' as in?"

"I don't know, I've never been," she replies, making me laugh. This girl is a mess of her own making.

"Well, I guess we're going to find out."

"Yes, we are. Tomorrow is our day, Bell. We are going to make them our bitches," she giggles, making me laugh along with her.

"You think we should see what to wear? Like, ask Ryan?"

"Why the hell would we ask Ryan? He has no sense of fashion. I think we should go looking like hookers."

"Hookers?"

"Yes, hookers. Make us look available. We don't want to go in there wearing something that doesn't show us off," she reasons.

"I suppose that makes sense, although I don't plan on sleeping with any of them," I tell her.

"Why the hell not? Isn't that the whole point?"

"For you, maybe. Not for me."

"I plan on getting all the dick I can get. It's been a while for me. I know for a fact that it's been a while for you too."

"Don't compare our sex lives. Mine is seriously lacking."

"I know that, which is why you should get you some tomorrow, girl. There's been a dry spell."

"I always have a dry spell. It's my life, Ruby."

"Stop. No more of that downer shit. We're going to have a great time and hang out, dance, drink, and all that shit. They're bikers. They have to have liquor, right?"

"Your brother seems to."

"Truth. Which means everyone else will too."

"Are you sure they aren't rivals or friends or some shit? If Ryan finds out you were there, he's going to flip his shit," I remind her. I don't know if they are friends or if Ryan will find out that we were there, but I don't want Ruby in any trouble.

"I think it's fine. We're big girls. We can handle ourselves."

"Says the girl that called him before the cops," I mumble.

"Hey, that was different. We had a stalker," she argues, making me smile.

"You're right. Completely different," I add.

"Exactly. Now let's finish our food so we can go home   and   pick   out   our   outfits."

Chapter Seven

Cowboy

The party is going great, and I couldn't be happier. There are women basically throwing themselves at us as we drink and chill.

"You havin' a good time?" I ask one of the girls who currently has my cock in her mouth. She moans around it, and I growl low in my throat.

I toss back another shot, setting the glass back on the table in front of me. Her head bobs up and down until all hell breaks loose.

I hear screaming coming from the front doors and shove the girl away from me, tucking my cock back into jeans as I stand to my feet. Shade and I share a glance when we see Tyrant and Mav heading that way. Shade nods his head, and we both follow behind them toward the door.

"What the hell?" I mumble when the screaming gets louder.

"We need to see Cowboy!" I know that voice. I shove through the crowd to see Ruby standing there.

"What the hell are you doin' here?" I growl at her. Everyone turns to look at me before Tyrant speaks.

"You know her?"

"That's my sister. What the fuck are you doin' here, Ruby?" I grab her arm when I realize she isn't alone. Bell looks down, her hair hanging around her face so that I can't see it, but it's the red in her hair that pulls my attention.

"What the fuck happened?" I shove past Ruby and lift Bell's face slowly in my hand when I see it. Her eye is black, lips bleeding. There's blood in her hair and tears streaming down her cheeks.

"We went to a party," Ruby quickly answers as everyone slowly leaves the area. Everyone except the guys.

"What the hell is goin' on?" Mav asks, looking between all of us. I don't even know what the hell is going on.

"What happened to her face?" I ask, looking to Ruby for an answer.

"We went to a party, and something happened to her. I don't know, Ryan!"

"You don't know? What the hell kind of party were you at?"

"I club like yours! I heard some girls talking about it, and we dropped in. Everything was good until I saw her crying and bleeding."

"A club like mine? A fuckin' MC? You went to another MC? Are you fuckin' crazy?"

"I didn't know!" Ruby screams back at me. I pull my hand away from Bell's face and run it over mine. What the hell did they do to her? Where were they?

"Get them inside, Cowboy." Tyrant orders. I nod my head and usher the girls in, keeping Bell close to me. I don't know what the hell happened to her or who did this. I'm pissed, on edge, and half-drunk.

"Come on," I tell the two of them, leading them down the hallway to one of the empty rooms we don't use. I sit Bell down in the first chair I come to when one of the club girls walks in.

"You need anything?" she asks, being too flirty for the fucking situation.

"Yeah, rags and water," I tell her. She rolls her eyes but walks back out of the room, going for the stuff I need.

"You wanna tell me what the hell happened?" I look to Ruby as she holds her shirt together. Fire races through my veins at the thought of anyone hurting my sister.

"Did they … Did someone …" I can't even finish the sentence. Ruby shakes her head, but her eyes fall on Bell. "Get out of the room, Ruby."

"What? No. I'm not leaving her."

"I said get out! Get the hell out of here!" My anger is palpable, and Ruby can feel it. She quickly walks out of the room, closing the door behind her. I kneel in front of Bell, brushing the hair away from her face.

"Tell me what happened."

"We were partying like she said. She was having a good time, and so was I. Then things changed. This guy … he kissed me. It was fine until some girl jumped me. Once one started, the other's joined in."

"You were jumped?"

"Yeah. I guess it was her boyfriend. I don't know, Ryan. It all happened so fast," she tells me. My stomach sinks. It could have been a lot worse. Things could have gone in a different direction. Those girls could have killed her, and no one would have batted a fucking eye.

"Fuck, Bell. What were you two thinkin'?"

"She wanted to know what it was like! So did I. We just showed up, and everything was fine."

"But it didn't end fine. You see this shit? You see yourself?" I roar. She flinches and leans back in her seat, eyeing me like I was in the wrong.

"I got jumped. I'll live."

"Your face is fucked. You probably have a concussion."

"All things I'll recover from."

"You sound just like her," I grumble under my breath. Ruby is rubbing off on this girl, and I don't know if I like it or not.

"She's my best friend. I couldn't have said no."

"You serious right now?" I ask.

"Yeah, I am. You don't get what it's like for people like us, Ryan."

The door opens, and the club girl Ally walks back in with the supplies I asked for. She sets them on the table and stares at me with lust in her eyes.

"Not happenin', Ally." She huffs and walks back out of the room as I watch her ass. Bell huffs out a breath that catches my attention.

"What?"

"Nothing. I was wondering what all this club shit was about, and now I can see. It's all about the girls. Whose pussy you can get," she snaps as if she's mad.

"Is that right? That's what you found out?"

"That's exactly what I found out."

"Then you have no fuckin' idea what you're talkin' about," I tell her as I reach for the wet rag and bring it to her face.

"Oh, come on, Cowboy. I'm sure I know how you got that name." She isn't wrong there. I get so much ass that's why they called me that. It doesn't change anything, though.

"It's from fucking girls, isn't it?" She sounds disgusted, and maybe she has a right to be. I don't care what she thinks about me, though. Bell doesn't know me. The real me.

"What's the difference?"

"There is no difference. It doesn't matter. I can't believe I actually thought …" Bell doesn't finish her sentence, and I don't care to know why. I wipe her face, cleaning the blood off as she winces and tries to pull away.

"Did they do anything else to you? The guys, I mean."

"I wasn't raped if that's what you're asking."

"That's what I'm askin', Bell."

"Well, don't worry, that didn't happen."

"You're lucky. It could have been a lot worse. You two were stupid for goin' there."

"We just wanted to party. I didn't hear you inviting us," she sneers at me. I pull the rag away from her face and lower it.

"Are you fuckin' kiddin' me right now? You wanted to party here? Didn't you see what happens?"

"Is that what happens here, too?" she asks softly.

"No. We don't let our girls act like that."

"Don't let them?"

"That's right. They follow fuckin' directions here. What club were you at?" I ask, needing to change the subject.

"Hells Howlers."

"Are you fuckin' kiddin' me?" I snap loudly before shoving to my feet. Just as I reach the door, it opens, and Ty walks in. He looks between the two of us before he speaks.

"Who was it?"

"Howlers MC," I tell him. I can see the anger in his eyes before he sighs and runs his hand through his hair.

"Your sister is worried about her friend."

"She's fine. Stupid but fine."

"Excuse the fuck out of me?" Bell screeches.

"You heard me. You're stupid. You should have never have gone there!"

"We were trying to have a little fun, Ryan!" she shouts at me. She wanted fun? I can give her ass fun. Bending her over this table and fucking her senseless would be fun.

"And did you have fun, Bell? Looks like you had a great time tonight."

"Fuck you!"

"You wish," I hiss in her direction. I try to ignore the rage simmering below the surface. I want nothing more than to snap their necks for being so reckless. They shouldn't have gone there looking for a good time. They shouldn't have gone out at all.

"I'm leaving. I don't need this shit," she announces, standing to her feet. Like hell she is. This isn't over.

"You're not goin' anywhere."

"Yes, I am. I'm going home," she snaps at me once more. I want to grab her, wrap my hand around her throat and make her understand what the hell I'm saying to her. She's so far out of her fucking league here.

"I said you're stayin' right where you are."

"Why are you interrogating me? Why aren't you bitching at your sister?" It makes sense, I should be all over Ruby, but after what I felt the other night with Bell, I can't get the girl out of my head. And Ruby seemed fine. She didn't seem hurt like Bell is.

"I got her ass next."

"Get her ass first. I'm done."

"We're far from done here, Bell."

"What do you want me to tell your sister?" Ty asks, interrupting our showdown.

"Tell her I'll be with her in a minute. Have one of the girls get her a shirt out of my room," I say to him, keeping my eyes pinned to Bell's. There's no way in hell that I'm going to let this go. She could have been hurt a hell of a lot worse than she was.

"Got it." Ty turns and leaves the room when I stalk toward the door. I flip the lock and turn back to her, my eyes and body on fire.

"Did they touch you?"

"What? Who?"

"Any of them. You were grindin' that pussy of yours all over them. Did they touch you?" Bell begins to open her mouth as I slowly stalk toward her. She's my goddamn prey. She's what I want, and I'm going to take her. I don't care if she protests.

"We were dancing," she answers finally after a long pause.

"Did he touch your pussy?" I demand this time. She slowly shakes her head as I step up in front of her. I move my hand, gripping her pussy through her jeans as she glares up at me.

"What are you doing?"

"Did they put their hands here?" She shakes her head once more. I want to lick her, suck her clit, and fuck her hard. I want to turn her around and make her mine right here and now. I shouldn't do it. I should let her walk away, but I can't.

"No."

"Good. No one's hand should be here but mine, Annabell." Her eyes narrow as she looks me in the eye, but she doesn't say a word. She just stares at me with her lips parted slightly. How easy it would be for me to slip my tongue into her mouth and taste her right now.

"I want these jeans off and on the floor now." It's an order. One she better follow as I step back and pull my jeans down. She watches me but doesn't move, and that's when I clear my throat. When she still doesn't move, I reach for her and pop the button on her jeans myself. I strip her out of her jeans and panties before turning her to face away from me.

"Are you on somethin'?"

"Yes."

"Good." I step in behind her and shove her over the table in front of her. Her hands are splayed out on the table while I massage her ass in my hands. Before she can protest, I shove into her. I wrap my free hand up in her hair and tug her head back, leaning over her to caress her neck with my lips.

"You were bad, Bell. You don't listen," I whisper in her ear, feeling her pussy clench around me. I groan and thrust into her.

"So bad," she whispers as I fuck her harder. My hips roll, taking her hard and fast. I pull out only to slam back into her over and over again. She pants, crying my name, and begs for more. I give it to her too.

"You gonna be bad again, Bell?" I ask her as I thrust harder.

"Maybe," she cries as I slam into her. My heart jackhammers in my chest the faster I take her. Letting her hair go, I grab her hips in my hands and fuck her good. When she clenches and begins to pant faster, I know she's close. My balls tighten, a tingle shooting through my body until I feel her come undone. I follow, releasing inside of her like a goddamn freight train.

Chapter Eight

Annabell

My body aches, but in a good way from what Ryan did to me in there. I should have stopped him, but I didn't want to. I wanted to feel what he did to me. I wanted to feel something after the night I'd had.

He's currently ripping Ruby a new ass as I sit on his bed watching them. Ruby doesn't take his shit, though. Instead, she gives it right back.

"You're stupid, Ruby."

"And you're a prick. You should have invited us here," she argues, crossing her arms over her chest.

"You don't belong here," he shoots back at her, mimicking her stance.

"Neither do you, but here you are. And why did you fuck my friend? Don't even act like no one heard that shit happening." I feel my cheeks heat as she talks about me, but she doesn't look my way. Is she mad at me? Does she hate me for letting him do it?

"That's none of your business."

"Neither is why we were at that club," she responds.

"Ruby, don't you dare fuck with me right now. I'm pissed at you."

"And I think you're overreacting."

"Look at her face! Do you know what they could have done to her?" he roars, scaring the shit out of me. I jolt and scoot back on the bed a little further.

"We were fine. I helped fight those girls off," Ruby says, which is true. She did help fight them off, but they were clearly out for blood. Mine.

"So that makes it all okay then? That's how you want to play this?"

"What do you want me to say? I'm sorry my best friend got hurt, Ryan! I'm sorry that she's still hurting, but we just wanted to have a little fun," Ruby whines before turning her gaze to meet mine. "I'm sorry, Bell."

"You're in the next room over. Shade has some clothes for you to change into," Ryan finally tells her. She nods her head, looking heartbroken, before she walks out of the room and closes the door behind her. Ryan turns to face me, and I can see the anger in his eyes.

"You didn't have to be so mean to her."

"I should have been a lot worse to her. You have no idea what you guys were up against."

"Other girls. I lost."

"You could have been killed."

"I wasn't, though."

"You could have been!" he thunders. I watch him walk around the room, grabbing a bottle off the dresser and unscrewing the cap. He brings it to his lips before taking one last look at me. Then he's back out the door like nothing happened, slamming it as he goes.

I look around the room before I become too exhausted to sit here any longer. Then I pull the blanket back and climb under, curling into a ball. The pillow and sheets smell like Ryan. I close my eyes and doze off almost immediately.

I'm awoken sometime later to noises in the dark room. Blinking rapidly, I try to find the source, but it's so dark in here. Then I hear a woman giggling, and vomit rises in my throat. Did he bring another girl in here with me in here? How dare he do that!

"What the fuck is going on?" I ask loudly when the light flips on. I shield my eyes, letting them adjust to the light for a second when I see Ryan with a completely naked girl wrapped around him. My stomach rolls as I take them in. His hand is around her back, holding onto her hip as they stumble through the room.

"Bell. Shit, you're really here," he slurs as he looks at me with glossy eyes.

"You told me to stay here," I remind him.

"I did? Well shit. This is awkward, isn't it?" he chuckles. Ignoring the need to slap the fuck out of the two of them, I climb out of bed and grab my shoes, heading for the door. That's when Ryan stops me. His arm shoots out, hooking me around the waist before pulling me back into him. His hard body gives off so much heat I can hardly stand it, but it's the look of lust in his eyes that pisses me off. He can't seriously think he's having both of us.

"Let me go, Ryan," I tell him trying to pry his hand off me. Unfortunately, he's stronger than me, and his grip stays.

"I don't think so. You're here," he mumbles once more as if that wasn't obvious to begin with.

"And now I'm leaving."

"Let her leave, Cowboy," the girl slurs as she saunters over and lowers herself onto his bed.

"You get out. Bell's here," he orders, nodding toward the door. I roll my eyes internally, cursing myself for staying here. I can't believe he brought some girl back to his room knowing I was in here. The thought makes me sick to my stomach.

"Cowboy," she whines, and I roll my eyes once more. I can't deal with whiny drunk bitches. I'm too tired for that shit.

"I said get out." I watch her shove off the bed and stroll toward the door before she finally walks out and slams it behind her. Petty bitch.

"Can I go now?" I ask Ryan.

"No. You can't go now. Get back in bed. I woke you up, didn't I?"

"I'm not going back to bed with you, Ryan. You brought some girl in here."

"So what? I didn't fuck her," he reasons. No, he fucked me before we got in this room. What kind of man is he? I thought he was different, but clearly, I was wrong.

"You were going to! Just let me go and find Ruby. I'll sleep with her," I tell him again.

"No. You sleep here, Bell!"

"Fine. Then let's go to sleep, and that's all we're doing."

"No fuckin'? My cock's hard as a rock, though," he whines as I walk toward the bed. I climb back in, pull the blankets up over me, and close my eyes as I listen to Ryan rummage through his drawers. Finally, after what seems like forever, he climbs in the bed with me. The next thing I know, he has me in his arms, kissing my neck before snuggling against me.

His leg wraps around mine, and within seconds he's snoring softly in my ear.

I lie here for a long time, debating pulling away from him. I should go and find Ruby, but she's probably already asleep.

Instead of doing that, I snuggle into the pillow and Ryan's warmth and doze off again into a peaceful sleep.

Chapter Nine

Cowboy

My head pounds as I snuggle closer to whoever it is in my bed. I don't remember much from last night, but I remember drinking until I couldn't see straight. I was beyond pissed at Ruby and Bell. I couldn't believe what they'd done and then showed up here looking how they did. My anger was off the charts.

I breathe in the scent of the girl curled up in my arms when it hits me. This isn't just some girl. It's Bell. Did I fuck her again? Did I take her last night after I got drunk? Fuck me. I can't remember shit but feeling her this close to me is the best feeling I've had in a long time.

Her soft breaths fan across my chest as I pull her in closer. Her hair is fanned out on the pillow behind her, looking like a goddamn goddess, and she's in my fucking bed. I know this is all kinds of messed up. I shouldn't have done what I did before I got drunk, but she had me so wound up it wasn't even funny. My hands itched to spank her ass, marking it red. My cock begged to be inside of her like it is right now. The hard length pressed against her stomach. It would be so easy to roll her over and slip inside of her once more. So fucking easy, but I can't do that. I've already crossed a line with her that I shouldn't have. She shouldn't be here in my bed or my arms, for that matter.

She sighs in her sleep, causing bumps to form over my flesh. How the hell am I going to keep my cock out of her now that I know what she feels like?

"Ryan?" she whispers as I pull her in closer, as close as I can get her.

"Hmm."

"You're suffocating me." I let out a chuckle and let her pull away from me. I shouldn't be holding onto her like that anyway. Fuck, my head is a pounding mess.

Bell scoots across the bed as far as she can get when her eyes open and lock with mine.

"That bruise is pretty bad," I tell her, lifting my hand to run my fingers along her cheek. She winces, and I almost pull away, but I can't.

"We can't do this," she says.

"I know. You don't belong here," I tell her truthfully. She doesn't belong in this lifestyle. Bell would be eaten up and spat back out. She's a good girl, not the kind that ends up with a guy like me.

"Yet I'm here."

"That changes today. I'm gonna make sure everything is good, and then you're goin' home."

"Kicking me out already?"

"I'm no good for you, Bell. We both know that," I tell her.

"I know."

"Then it's settled. It won't happen again."

"What if I liked it?" she asks, causing my dick to stir once more.

"Doesn't matter. It's over now."

"Is it?" she asks as she pulls the blanket off my naked body. She slowly climbs down the bed and grabs my cock in her soft little hand before stroking it a few times. That motherfucker comes to life just like I knew he would. Then I feel her lips wrap around the tip.

"I just said no," I tell her, but she doesn't listen. Her tongue flattens along my cock as she sucks me deeper into her mouth. I can't fight her. I don't want to. Instead, I raise my hips and fuck her mouth. Bell bobs her head, taking me deeper with each thrust of my hips until I'm hitting the back of her throat. She doesn't even fucking gag; she just keeps sucking. I let her take over and do her thing until I feel that familiar tingle run down my spine.

"I'm gonna come, Bell. Let me pull out," I warn her, but she doesn't stop. She keeps going until I blow down the back of her throat. Bell eagerly swallows me whole until there is nothing left in me. When I pull out of her mouth, she gazes up at me with a twinkle in her eyes.

"Now it's done."

"You wanted to suck my cock?" I ask, confused by what she's saying.

"Yeah. I've kinda had a thing for you." Her admission runs straight through me. I watch her climb out of bed wearing one of the t-shirts I left for her to change into. It makes me overthink things. It makes me question everything I just said to her.

"You could have worn shorts, you know?"

"Why?" she asks as she bends over so I can see just what I'm missing out on. I groan and roll onto my back, pulling my eyes away from the sight in front of me. I listen to the rustle of her clothing as she gets dressed before I glance back over at her.

"Thanks for letting us stay last night," her voice is soft. I throw the blanket off me and climb out of bed, walking my naked ass over to the dresser for clean clothes. My head is still pounding as I pull my boxers and jeans on. I leave them unbuttoned, hanging loosely from my waist, when I finally turn to face her.

"Let me see your face."

"It's fine."

"Let me see it, Bell." She lets out a sigh before walking toward me. I raise my hand and run it along her cheek as I check the swelling around her eye.

"You need to wash your hair," I tell her. "There's a lot of blood stuck in it."

"I will, at home."

"I have a shower in there," I point to the bathroom.

"You made it clear that we were finished," she tells me.

"That doesn't mean you can't take a shower, Bell."

"Yeah, it kind of does. Where's Ruby?"

"She's in the room next door."

"And your slut?"

"My what?"

"The slut you thought you were having fun with last night." I rub the back of my neck as I try to remember who the hell I brought in here last night. I can't think, but clearly, she didn't stick around.

"I don't even remember that," I admit to her.

"Clearly."

"What's that supposed to mean?"

"Nothing. Can I go now, Dad? Is this interrogation over?"

"Don't call me dad. Call me daddy," I smile at her. She doesn't smile back, just rolls her eyes.

"I'm going to find Ruby."

"You think you're going to walk around the clubhouse alone?"

"Why not? You said you weren't like them."

"We're not, but that doesn't mean the guys can keep their hands to themselves. Come on," I usher her out the door.

"Shouldn't you put clothes on?"

"Why?"

"You know. In case the skanks can't keep their hands to themselves."

"Are you jealous? Say you're jealous, and I'll put a shirt on," I tell her as we walk down the hallway.

"I'm not jealous. Have fun with that," she responds as we walk into the main room. I look around and see the guys standing or sitting around. They glance over when we walk into the room, but that's about it. I don't have any worries that any of the guys would touch Bell or hurt her like she was last night. I just didn't want her out here by herself. Maybe I'm an asshole or a prick, but I want them to know she was with me last night. I want them to know she's off-limits.

"Where's Ruby?" I ask Ty when I see him standing near the bar. He nods his head toward the corner where I see her smiling and hanging off Shade. Oh, like fuck, she is.

"Ruby!" She jerks and whips her head around in my direction when a smile creeps across her face.

"Hey, bro."

"Get your ass over here," I snap at her. She laughs, throwing her head back before saying something to Shade and patting his arm. Then she slides off the stool and strolls toward me like she doesn't have a care in the world.

"What's with the demands?"

"What the hell are you doin' with Shade?"

"He's so nice, Ryan. I didn't realize your club was so nice." Her answer makes me cringe. That means she will want to hang out around here, and that's not going to happen.

"I think now's a good time to bring this up. If you wanna party, I think this should be your new spot. No more hittin' up random MC's." Tyrant's words have my head snapping in his direction, my eyes nearly bugging out of my head.

"What the hell are you sayin'?" I ask him.

"That they should party here where you can keep an eye on them."

"What the fuck, Ty?" I snap at him.

"It makes sense, Cowboy. They don't need to be out there fuckin' round and gettin' hurt again or worse. I think it's for the best."

"Yeah, he thinks it's for the best, and I really appreciate that, Tyrant," Ruby says, smiling up at him. He nods his head and turns, walking away, leaving me with the two of them.

"So, you fucked her."

"Shut up, Ruby."

"Well, you did. I know my best friend. She was fucked last night," she says again. I ignore her and grab a beer from behind the bar before she looks at me. No, she stares at me.

"What?"

"Well, did you?"

"Why are you askin' me and not her?" I nod toward Bell. She just crosses her arms over her chest and glares at me.

"Yeah, tell her, Cowboy."

"What the fuck is this? Bust my nuts day? I let you two stay here last night, and this is what I get?" I'm not really annoyed with them, but I don't plan on telling my sister that I fucked her best friend last night and got the most amazing bj this morning either. That's none of her business.

"Oh, come on. Spit it out, Ryan! Or did she spit?"

"Go the hell home. I can't handle any more of you," I tell her.

"But you can handle more of Bell?" she asks, raising her eyebrow.

This is hell. I'm living in the middle of hell.

Chapter Ten

Annabell

"So you and my brother," Ruby says for the hundredth time today. I can't make her stop. She just keeps going.

"It was an angry fuck. I don't think he even liked it," I repeat.

"Angry fucks are the best ones."

"Why don't we talk about the fact that you were huddled up with Shade this morning."

"We didn't fuck, though. I mean, I tried to get him to, but he wouldn't. The man must be a saint because I was grinding and everything on his cock."

"You're sick. You do know that, right?"

"I know. I can't help it. It's a curse. But you did fuck my brother and sleep in his room," she points out while pointing at me. I shake my head, running my hand through my now clean hair.

"He cuddles, Ruby. He's a fucking cuddler."

"No way! Ryan doesn't cuddle!"

"I'm telling you he was cuddling me. It was suffocating me. Your brother is totally a cuddler."

"My god, I would have never thought of him like that. He's always so hard and rough around the edges. To find out the prick has a soft side is interesting and adds ammo to my arsenal."

"Leave the man alone. I didn't tell you so you could torment him."

"Then why did you tell me?"

"I don't know! It slipped?"

"Did not. You like my brother, don't you?" I sigh. I should have told her this a long time ago, but I didn't. I should have told her I had a crush on him when I was younger.

"I've always liked Ryan. I kinda had a thing for him when we were younger. It's weird that I haven't seen him in years and then bam, it's still there."

"You're still crushing on him? You're going to be my sister-in-law?" she coos.

"Shut up. I am not. It was just one time."

"But you liked it."

"I'm not discussing that with you. It's weird and gross all at the same time," I remind Ruby. This is her brother we're talking about.

"Wonder if he likes you too? I think we should drop by the clubhouse. See what they're doing."

"Why would we?" I ask.

"Tyrant said we could come over anytime we wanted to."

"You have a good point. Are you driving, or should I?"

"See! You want my brother!"

"I want to see what they do all day. In case you forgot, we were locked in rooms the entire night, and we didn't get to see anything." We never got to leave the room that night, not until morning, and we were ushered out of there.

"Good point. Let's go," she stands to her feet before grabbing my hands and pulling me up. I follow her out to the car and climb in as she starts the engine. Then she's pulling out onto the street like a bat out of hell. We're a few minutes into our drive when I notice a car still behind us. I try to ignore it, and I sure as hell don't tell Ruby about it. I don't want her to freak out on me.

"You sure this is smart?" I ask as an afterthought. Maybe we shouldn't just show up there. Or maybe we should, now that there's a weird car behind us.

"Of course, this is smart." The drive only takes a few more minutes when we're pulling into the parking lot. I let out a sigh of relief when I see the car stop for only a second and take off again.

Ruby is out of the car in seconds heading for the door as I rush to keep up with her. When we walk in, she takes off toward the bar as I glance around to see who is here. That's when I spot Tyrant off to the side. I stroll over, acting like I belong, when his head tips up and his eyes lock with mine.

"What happened?"

"Um, I really don't know. Ruby wanted to come here, and there was a car following us. She didn't pay much attention to it," I tell him when he cuts me off.

"What kind of car? What color?"

"A black car. I don't know what kind. An SUV, it looked like."

"Stay here. Don't fuckin' move." I nod my head as he walks over to another guy and says something. The guy nods his head and takes off toward the back of the clubhouse. Tyrant turns and walks back over to me.

"How far did they follow you?"

"All the way here. They slowed down out front but then took off."

"Walk with me," he commands, not giving me the option. I turn and follow him down the hallway into a side room where the guy he was talking to a minute ago sits at the computer. His fingers move effortlessly over the keys as I watch the screen.

"That one!" I say when I see the car on the screen. "It was that one."

"Fake tag," the guy mumbles as his finger continues to move over the keyboard. "Could be anyone."

"You have anyone that you pissed off?" Tyrant asks.

"Besides the Howlers girls? No."

"It wasn't them. They wouldn't have come in a car. They would have been on bikes."

"Unless they planned to kidnap them," the guy adds.

"Shut up, Les. They weren't plannin' to kidnap anyone, or they would have grabbed them comin' out of the apartments."

"So, who do you think it was?"

"Hard to say," he replies, running a hand through his hair. "What are you doin' here anyway?"

"You said we could come anytime." I shrug my shoulders because I don't know what else to say. We're nosey bitches? I couldn't tell him that.

"You're right, I did. Fuck!"

"We can leave."

"No, you can't. Cowboy isn't here yet. You're gonna have to wait on him," he says.

"Who the hell said I came to see him?" He turns his head to stare down at me, an intense look in his eyes.

"Who the hell are you here to see then?"

"No one."

"Lies."

"Ruby wanted to see Shade," I shrug.

"For fucks sake."

"What? He's not a good guy or what?" I find myself asking. I need to know what my friend is getting herself into.

"He's fine. Just not what Cowboy had in mind for his little sister."

"Which is what?"

"A normal man."

"Yo, Prez. The guys are back," someone calls out. Ty heads for the door with me right behind him. I follow him out into the main room when I see Ryan. He's standing there, a smug grin on his face, blood on his hands. That is blood isn't it?

"Shit's handled, brother."

"No one saw you?"

"Hell no, no one saw me," Ryan says with that same smirk on his face.

"Good. We got another issue."

"What's that?" Ryan asks when Tyrant turns and nods toward me. Ryan's eyes flash dark before he blinks and looks at me once more.

"The fuck is this?" he asks, looking back toward Tyrant.

"They showed up."

"They? Where the fuck is Ruby?"

"She's with Shade," I announce. Tyrant lets out a chuckle, but Ryan looks deadly.

"Get my goddamn sister away from him and corral them till I get out of the shower," Ryan tells him. Tyrant nods his head and turns around to face me, a smirk plastered across his face.

"You heard the man. Get the fuck over here and sit down."

"You're not my boss."

"You're in my clubhouse, sweetheart. That means I can tell you what I want and when I want it. Now, get that pretty little ass over here and sit down." Tyrant's voice was a little harder than before. I huff out a breath and stomp over, sitting in the chair he's pointing to while Ryan walks through the room cursing under his breath. It's almost funny to see him all frazzled the way he is.

"Can I at least get a drink?" I risk asking.

"Prospect! Get the girl a drink!" I watch the guy move quickly behind the bar and grab a drink before I can even blink.

"Isn't that a little rude?" I ask.

"No. It's his job. Now sit here with your drink and be quiet while I find Ruby."

"Fine." I huff out a breath and sit back in my chair.

Chapter Eleven

Cowboy

"Was that blood on your hands?"

"Maybe, and if you don't shut up, it might be yours next." Bell rolls her eyes, leans back in her seat, and huffs out a breath.

"Are you mad that we're here? We can leave."

"I know you can, and you're goin' to soon," I tell her. I can't believe they showed up here. I should have known better, especially where my sister is concerned. Once Tyrant invited them back, she wouldn't stay away now.

"Why not now?"

"There's a situation, that's why." One that we need to handle, but it looks like the situation is coming to us. Tyrant is busy making plans while I'm sitting here trying to remain calm, knowing what's about to happen. I entrusted Shade with Ruby, but that doesn't mean this is sitting well with me. It's not. I glance over and see them in the corner of the room when I give him a nod. I want her out of sight in the next two minutes. I raise my two fingers for him to see, and he nods his head.

"Hey, Cowboy, you ready?"

"Yeah. Where are they?"

"A few minutes out. You should probably head back with her." I nod my head at Maverick before standing and grabbing Bell's hand. I pull her out of the chair and lead her up the stairs toward my room. I know Shade is right behind me with Ruby.

"What are we doing?" she asks when I shove her inside.

"There's a situation," I tell her as I check the windows are closed and locked.

"No shit. You said that."

"What are we doing in here?" Ruby asks as soon as Shade leads her into the room.

"Shit's about to get real. I'm gonna need you to stay in this room no matter what you hear."

"What the hell does that mean?" Bell snaps at me. I'm not in the mood or the right state of mind to deal with this shit today. So instead, I spin around on her, grabbing her around the throat before pushing her against the closest wall.

"It means shit is about to go south for the club. It means we're about to be attacked. So, when I say stay the hell in this room and be quiet, I mean it. Don't fuck with me right now, Bell." Her eyes are wide as the words leave my mouth. Ruby gasps, and Shade just nods his head. They don't know what to expect, and frankly, neither do we. We've never had anyone come at us at our clubhouse before, so this is all new to us too. We just got word that a rival was heading our direction.

"Are they going to kill us?" Bell asks, her eyes wild. I lean down, kiss her gently and shake my head.

"No. Now stay here." She nods her head, and I release my hold on her. Stepping back, I see the way she huddles into herself. Shade is whispering something in Ruby's ear, and she nods her head before looking to Bell. Then the two of us leave them huddled together before heading out in the hallway.

"This is bullshit," Shade tells me.

"No shit. I can't believe they are comin' at us like this," I tell him.

"At our fuckin' clubhouse at that. What kinds of shit are they tryin' to pull?" he hisses as we walk down the steps and back into the main room.

"I don't know, but we're about to find out."

"Where do you want us?" I ask Tyrant as the guys all scramble around the room, getting ready for god only knows what.

"Out front. We got the back covered and upstairs too." I nod my head, pull my gun and flick off the safety before heading out the front door. I stand tall and ready for whatever is coming our way.

I hear the rumble of bikes in the distance. The closer the bikes get, the harder my heart beats. I can hear the blood roaring in my ears as rage fuels my blood. They won't win, whoever the hell they are. They won't get past us.

The rumbles become closer until I can see the bikes coming down the road. I glance to my right at Maverick, then left at Tyrant. Shade and I stand in front of the doors, waiting. Guys are lined all around the clubhouse. Anyone who dared to try and get in would be killed first.

"Get ready!" Tyrant calls out. He no sooner finishes speaking when shots are fired. We return fire as the bikes loop around and a van pulls into view. The side door slides open and more men are hanging out of the open door, shooting at us. We duck, take cover, and fire back. A few go down, but their guys are quick to pick them up and load them into the van.

"Shoot the bastards!" Tyrant roars as more shots ring out through the night. The bikes retreat along with the van until there is no one or nothing in sight. Our clubhouse sits off the road, so there are no other people around. Right now, I'm thanking God for that.

"They're gone. You see the cuts?"

"Howlers MC, Tyrant," Shade replies through a growl.

"Fuck!" I roar. What the hell are they doing? Are they after the girls or us?

"You gotta be shittin' me!" Tyrant yells into the night. "Check inside!"

I turn on my heel and head back inside, seeing the bullet holes that riddle the clubhouse. I rush through the main room and up the stairs, shoving past a few guys, heading straight for my room. When I get inside, I see the girls huddled on the floor crying.

"You two good? No one was hit?" I ask, looking between the two of them. Ruby points to a spot right above her head and cries.

"It was so close. I-I could feel it go past," she cries harder. I rush over and drop to my knees, pulling them both into my arms.

"You're okay. Everything's okay now." I can't be sure of that. Not yet, but I need them to think that, believe that. I don't need them freaking out on me right now.

"It was so close, if Bell was just a little closer. Oh my god, Ryan. It would have killed her," Ruby sobs. I pull back a little and look at Bell, but her face is stark white. I know she's in shock, and there's nothing I can do to help her right now.

"Bell? Look at me." I tell her softly. Slowly she raises her head, and her fear-stricken eyes meet mine. "You're okay, Bell."

"I-it was so close. It was so loud," she whispers. I nod my head as Shade comes into the room and looks between all of us. I nod toward Ruby, and he walks over, pulling her from the floor and into his arms. I grab Bell and pull her against me, her body trembling.

"Everything's okay now. No one is gonna hurt you."

"They were after us?" she asks, shocked. Fuck.

"We don't know what they wanted. We got this, though. Don't worry."

"Don't worry? Don't worry?" she screams, shoving at my chest. I step back and give her the space she's trying to create before resting my hands on my hips.

"Yeah, don't worry."

"That bullet almost killed me! It almost went straight through my head, Cowboy!" She roars with anger and fear.

"I know that. You're okay, though," I remind her.

"Fuck you! Fuck you, Ryan! Fuck this clubhouse and whatever it is you motherfuckers do. Fuck all this. I'm getting the hell out of here." Before I know it, she's heading for the door, but I know the guys aren't letting anyone out. The club went into lockdown.

"You gonna chase her?" Shade asks as he holds Ruby against him.

"No. She ain't goin' anywhere."

"Ryan?"

"Yeah?"

"Are we really okay?" Ruby asks. I walk over and pull my sister out of Shade's arms and into mine. I rest my head on top of hers.

"I'm not gonna let anyone hurt you, darlin'. I promise." Just as the words leave my mouth, I hear Bell screaming at the top of her lungs.

Chapter Twelve

Annabell

Guys block the door, and others stand with guns in hand. I scream at the asshole at the door, but he doesn't let me go.

"You can't leave right now, sweetheart. I'm sorry."

"Don't you call me that, you asshole. Let me the fuck out of here!" I scream louder this time. When he doesn't move, I look around and spot Ryan casually walking down the steps as if we weren't just shot at. How can he be so calm? Is this the kind of shit the club does? I can't be here. I can't stay here.

"You tell them to let me out, Ryan!" I'm almost shrieking now. He shakes his head, a smirk on his face as he walks our way.

"Can't do that. The club is in lockdown, darlin'."

"Don't call me little pet names and think it makes everything all better, you asshole."

"I'm not tryin' to make things better. Unfortunately, things are shit and about to get worse," he tells me as I see a few guys coming in with blood coating their flesh. One holds his arm while the other keeps pressure on another's stomach. My stomach rolls at the sight before focusing back on Ryan. I can't do this. I can't see this.

"I need to leave, Ryan. I can't be here."

"Do you know who was shooting at us?" he asks me. I look at him like he's lost his mind as I shake my head at him.

"No. How the hell would I know?"

"It was the Hells Howlers, Bell. It was the same fuckin' club you and my sister decided to visit."

"What? No." I shake my head, not believing this. What the hell would they want? Why would they do this? Are they after us?

"Yeah, it was them. Now I need you to calm down and come back to my room."

"That bullet almost killed me, Ryan!"

"I know, darlin'. I know." My insides tremble before I fall apart. Tears spring to my eyes before my legs give out. I fall to the floor, but Ryan is there to catch me. He pulls me into his arms and holds me tightly, but my body won't stop shaking.

"It was so close," I cry as he tries to calm me. I was almost killed. A few more inches and I wouldn't be here. Ryan keeps me held tightly, his lips caressing my cheek.

"I'm sorry. You shouldn't have been here," Ryan whispers against my flesh as he rocks me in his arms.

"We need to have church!" I hear someone yell, but I don't pay attention to who it was. I don't care.

"I'm gonna have the prospect take you back to Ruby, okay?"

"Don't leave me. Please," I beg.

"I'm not goin' anywhere, but I need to talk to the guys about this shit. I need you to go back upstairs with Ruby, yeah?" Reluctantly I nod my head as Ryan pulls us to our feet.

"Prospect!" he hollers. A younger guy comes over quickly and stands there waiting for instructions. Ryan tells him to take me back up to his room with his sister and not to leave us alone. The guy nods and motions for me to walk. I take one last look at Ryan before following his orders.

We walk back up the steps and down the hall heading back into Ryan's room. Ruby launches off the bed and comes running, wrapping me in her arms.

"Oh my god, Bell."

"I know."

"He'll fix this. I know he will."

"I know."

"Everything will be okay."

"He said it was the same club that we went to, Ruby. What if they're after us?"

"They couldn't be. We didn't do anything to them. We showed up and what happened happened. We didn't do anything wrong," she tries to reassure me.

"I know, but my god. How ironic is it that it's the same club?" I ask her. It's strange.

"It is strange, but they wouldn't know we were here. How would they? They don't know anything about us," she reminds me. She's right. They don't know us, and they don't know anything about us. We showed up once, and that was it.

"You're right. I'm just scared."

"I know. Me too. That was scary as hell," she says, pulling away from me.

"How is your brother so calm?"

"I don't know. I guess he's used to it." Used to it? This can't possibly be what the club does all the time.

"Used to it? Being shot at? This is what they do?"

"I don't know. I've never been invited here," Ruby reminds me. I'm uneasy. I walk over and sit on the edge of the bed, placing my hands in my lap. I pick at my nails when the door opens, and another guy walks in.

"We're gonna bring you some food. Anything you prefer?"

"Yes, we'd like a large pizza with mushrooms right after the big shoot-out!" Ruby yells at him.

"I'm just the messenger, darlin'."

"Well, tell my brother to fuck right off. We don't want to eat right now," she tells him. He smirks and starts to walk out of the room when I stop him. I need information.

"Is this what you guys do here? Does this happen often?"

"No. It doesn't happen often, but occasionally there will be some asshole who wants to try us."

"Try you? They shot at you!" I squeal.

"I'm well aware. Ain't the first time we've been shot at, sweetheart, and I'm sure it won't be the last. I'll let Cowboy know you didn't want anything."

"They do this often," I say as I look at Ruby.

"My brother is officially insane."

"He's beyond insane."

"You slept with the psycho!"

"He's your brother," I remind her. "You share DNA."

"Not by choice. This is insane. It's all insane. I want to go home," Ruby comes and sits next to me on the bed.

"Me too. I don't want to be here anymore." This place is crazy. I thought it was fun to party here, but now I see what happens; I don't want any part of it.

"You think my brother is really into this shit?" Ruby asks.

"You said he's been in the club for years. Obviously, he's into it. You're right; he's psychotic. I slept with a crazy man."

"You did."

"Way to be helpful."

"I try," she smiles at me.

We sit in silence for a long time before the door opens again, and Ryan walks in. This time he looks a little lost and disheveled. He walks past us, barely glancing at us before walking into the bathroom. Ruby and I share a look when she nods for me to go in there. I shake my head and nod for her to go.

"You go," she whispers.

"Hell no, it's your brother," I whisper back.

"You screwed him."

"And? You share blood!"

"I can fuckin' hear both of you, and I don't want either one of you in here." With that, we both shut our mouths and glance at each other.

A few minutes later, Ryan comes back out of the bathroom.

"You're both stayin' here for the next few days. Then, once we figure shit out, you can go home."

"A few days? We have class."

"Do it online. I don't give a shit. You're not leavin' until we have this sorted out."

"What was that, Ryan?" Ruby finally asks.

"We don't know yet. We're lookin' into it."

"You're looking into it? Shouldn't the cops be looking into it?"

"No. We handle our shit. Half the cops in this town belong to us."

"What the hell does that mean?"

"It means what I said, Ruby! Stop askin' questions you don't really want answers to," he snaps at her.

"What if we want the answers?" I ask. Ryan turns to us, his hands on his hips.

"You want the truth? You want to know why I kept you at a distance? This is why. This is my life. Don't you get that? We do illegal shit. We fuck with the wrong people, and this happens. People die, people get killed! You walked into a fuckin' warzone, and now I have to figure out how to protect your asses," he roars as he looks at us. Something swirls in my stomach, but it's Ruby who stands and rushes toward the bathroom. When I hear her throw up, I stand from the bed and walk over to Ryan.

"I don't want this," I tell him.

"You think I wanted this for you? Why do you think I haven't fucked with you in years, Bell? Why do you think I didn't drag Ruby around this place?" His eyes are on fire, and I can feel the blaze. I stupidly raise my hand and lay it against his chest. Ryan sucks in a breath before slowly exhaling.

"I'm sorry, Ryan."

"Don't be. I'm not. I enjoyed my time with you, Bell. If things were different …" He lets his sentence linger, but we both know what this is.

"I think I agree. If things were different, we could have worked. I like you, Ryan."

"I like you too, Bell. That's the reason I've kept you away, kept her away. I didn't want you two to see this side of me."

"But why do you do this?"

"It's my life. These guys are my family. I was never on the right side of the law, and we all knew it. This is it for me."

"What about me?"

"What about you?" he asks, breaking me apart. I really do care about him. I always have.

"This, whatever it is between us."

"It'd never work, but I can't stop thinkin' about you, Bell. You've fucked up my head a little," he chuckles lightly. He reaches up and wraps his fingers around my wrist, holding it tightly. My fingers are splayed across his chest before he lowers his head.

"This is a mistake," he whispers.

"Horrible mistake," I whisper back. Then his lips touch mine and everything else fades into the background. Why does he affect me this way? Why can't I think when he's this close to me?

"What is this?" Ruby asks when she walks out of the bathroom.

"This is me fuckin' up. I was prepared to let her go, but I lied. I'm not. You're mine, Bell. Fuck this shit. Fuck all the rest."

"I can't live like this," I tell him.

"I'm not givin' you the choice. Don't make me chase you because I will," he growls, taking me by surprise.

"You can't do this to her, Ryan."

"I can, and I will. In fact, I already did. So fight me on this, Bell. I wish you would."

"What the hell has gotten into you?" Ruby asks.

"She has! She has gotten into me. I'm sick of bein' alone. I'm tired of chasin' after club ass that doesn't mean shit to me." His words are like a slap to the face. I glance at Ruby, and I don't think she expected this from him either. She narrows her eyes before stepping closer and pulling us apart.

"We were just shot at, Ryan. Do you think any sane person wants to live like that?" she snaps at him.

"She isn't just any person. She's mine."

"She isn't yours. You've barely spent any time with her. You can't possibly feel anything for her," she argues.

"You can't tell me what I feel and when to feel it. If I said she's mine, then she's mine, Ruby. Drop it."

"Like fuck I will. She's my best friend," she reminds him.

"And you were fuckin' my best friend! What's the difference? You gettin' involved with Shade is no different than us, Ruby."

"Who the hell said I was involved with Shade?"

"Oh, come the fuck on. I saw the two of you. Don't give me that shit," he snaps at her.

"What about what I want?" I interrupt the two of them.

"What do you want, Bell?" Ryan asks as he watches me intently. Do I want him? Do I want to risk my life for a man? How can he promise to keep me safe when he doesn't even know what the hell is going on around here?

"I don't know."

"Tell me you don't want me, and I'll walk the fuck away. Say it!"

“I-I can’t.” I can’t say that because I do want him. I just don’t want this lifestyle, do I? Can I handle this?

Chapter Thirteen

Cowboy

What the fuck am I doing? What am I doing with her? I shouldn't be doing this, but I am. I'm claiming her whether she likes it or not. I don't care if she says no.

"You're delusional, Ryan!" Ruby snaps at me. I laugh it off because maybe I am. On the other hand, maybe I'm just that fucked up in the head.

"If that's how you feel. Come downstairs; we're eatin'."

"People were just shot! Are you fucking kidding me right now?" Ruby shouts in disbelief.

"I'm not kiddin' you, and you're gonna come down and eat before it's time for bed."

"I'm not doing anything," Ruby crosses her arms over her chest. I pull my cell out and dial Shade to come and deal with her ass. I have enough on my plate with Bell now.

"Just do what he says, Ruby," Bell says quietly.

"Finally, someone that can listen," I hiss.

"Oh, the only reason she's listening is because she wants to be fucked later. I, on the other hand, don't need to be so fuck you, Ryan. I can't believe this is the kind of shit you're involved in."

"Believe it, sis. This is my goddamn life. I tried to keep you out of it, but you were bound and determined to get your ass in here. Now you're here. Fuckin' deal with it."

"You can't force this on me, Ryan. I don't want this life."

"You did it to yourself. I kept you away."

"Fuck. Just fuck," Ruby mutters before lowering her head. I walk over and lift her chin so that she's looking at me.

"I didn't want this for you, but the fact is you're here. There's nothin' I can do to change that now."

"I'm sorry, Ryan. So fucking sorry," she sobs before wrapping her arms around my waist and resting her head on my chest. I hold her, letting her cry for a minute.

"It's not your fault. We think those guys were comin' for us before you two went there anyway. I just want to keep you safe until we figure it out for sure."

"Okay. I'll do whatever you say."

"Good. Let's go down and eat. Then we'll talk more." Ruby nods her head and wipes her eyes before grabbing Bell's hand. Shade comes through the door just as we begin to walk toward it.

"You needed me?"

"You called him to help you?" Bell asks with a little laugh.

"She didn't want to follow the rules. I think she's got it now," I answer him, nodding toward my sister. Shade's gaze falls on Ruby before he shakes his head and runs his hand through his hair.

"Foods here. Come eat." I nod my head and usher everyone out of my room before I walk over and run my finger over the bullet hole in the wall. It makes me sick to my fucking stomach to think that either one of them could have been hurt or worse.

"Fuck," I grumble under my breath. I turn and head for the door thanking God that they were safe.

I'm down the stairs and at the bar as the other girls serve the food. Ruby and Bell sit there awkwardly as one of the other old ladies talks to them. I can't make out what's being said, but I can see her hands moving animatedly. I'm sure she's trying to smooth over the whole shooting thing for them.

"You good brother?" Maverick asks me before sliding me a beer.

"That bullet came inches from one of them. Fuckin' inches."

"Goddamn, man. I didn't know," he shakes his head.

"I'll kill anyone who hurts those girls."

"I heard that. You got a thing with little sis's friend?"

"I basically claimed her ass upstairs. That a thing?" I ask him playfully. He chuckles and takes down his shot before passing me one. I take it and knock it back quick as fuck before chasing it with my beer.

"You claimed her, huh? She know what that means?"

"Not yet. I was savin' that for after dinner."

"That should make good conversation," he says.

"Yeah, we'll see about that shit." I walk over and take a seat on the other side of Ruby and grab some food, loading my plate. I know they're not used to this kind of thing, but I am, and I'm starving.

I take down my food and grab another beer as the guys talk shit about what happened. I stay silent for the most part, not wanting to scare the girls further.

"We're on lockdown for the next few days. That means no one out without my permission," Tyrant announces.

"I don't know about all of this," Ruby whispers.

"You don't need to know about it. Just calm down and let us handle it," I remind her. She nods her head and sits back in her chair, taking in everyone.

"Well, I don't think we should be staying here," Bell chimes in as she takes a bite of her food.

"And again, you don't have a choice. You're lucky I don't tie your ass to the bed."

"You wouldn't dare," she gasps. I turn my head to face her and grin.

"I think I'd like you tied to my bed and at my mercy. Maybe I'll get you fuckin' naked and kiss every inch of your body makin' you squirm. Maybe I'll lick that little clit of yours until your knees get weak and then make you beg to come." Her cheeks turn red as she looks at me with her mouth open. I want to lean in and suck her tongue into my mouth, but I don't. Instead, I turn back to my meal and finish eating.

When everyone is finished and the girls are cleaning up, I walk over to Tyrant at the bar and lean against it.

"You think this has anything to do with them?" I ask, nodding toward the girls.

"No. They wanted us out for a long time now. We just never made waves with them. Maybe they just decided to start a war," he replies. That's a slight relief.

"They wanna go home when this is over. You good with that?"

"A few days, Cowboy. Give me a few days, but yeah, that should be fine."

"Thanks, brother."

"Your sister is a wild one," he adds.

"No shit. This is why I didn't want her around this shit. She's mouthy and doesn't know when to stop."

"I heard that."

"She's about to be Shade's problem, though," I tell him, causing him to chuckle.

"What about the other one?"

"I claimed her ass upstairs. She's gonna be around more often," I admit, although I'm seriously rethinking my decision. I shouldn't have done that, but I want Bell. And I always get what I want.

"As long as you're ready for that."

"I gotta be now," I laugh.

"No shit," he adds.

"Thanks, brother."

I walk away from him and head toward the stairs, following where the girls went. They were going back to my room from what they said. When I walk in, I gasp at the sight in front of me. Bell is standing there in nothing but her bra and panties.

"You're stayin' like that," I say gruffly. She turns her head and looks over her shoulder at me before shaking her head and nodding toward the bathroom. Ruby must be in there. I reach down and adjust my cock before heading toward the dresser and pull a t-shirt free. I toss it to her watching the way her tits bounce as she moves. I lick my lips and wait for her to slide it over her head. After a minute, Ruby walks out of the bathroom and looks between the two of us.

"I'm sleeping in here tonight," she announces.

"You're on the couch then, and I'm fuckin' her senseless."

"You're sick, do you know that?" Ruby asks.

"I'm honest. There's a difference."

"I'm scared, Ryan."

"Shade will protect you," I tell her.

"Does it always come back to that? Maybe I just wanted a quick fuck. Did you ever think of that?"

"Now, who's the sick one?" I ask with a grin on my face.

"You're an asshole."

"And I'm still fuckin' her." Ruby covers her ears and acts like she doesn't hear me before walking over and dropping onto the bed. I watch as Bell follows her, climbing up on the bed next to her.

"They won't come back. They made their point," I tell them both.

"How do you know that?" Bell asks.

"Because that's how we work."

"What else do you do?" Ruby asks. I sigh because this wasn't a conversation that I wanted to have with my sister. I wasn't prepared for this shit.

"We sell guns to other clubs. Only clubs we're friendly with."

"You what?" Ruby blanches. She climbs to her knees on the bed before looking dead at me. "You can't be serious. This is dangerous, Ryan!"

"No shit. I think we all figured that out tonight, didn't we? It is what it is, Ruby."

"It is what it is? That's all you have to say? I can't believe my brother is a gun dealer."

"This is some shit you see on TV or in the movies," Bell adds.

"No, this shit is real life. You wanted to know, and now you do," I tell the two of them.

"I don't think I want to know anymore," Ruby says.

"Good. I didn't want to get into details with you. Just know in a few days you can go home."

"What about me?" Bell asks.

"You're gonna go home too, Bell, but be ready to see a lot more of me." She nods her head but looks down at her hands. Does she not want this? Want me? I can't think straight when I'm around this girl. I can't keep my head on straight. She drives me insane, and I know the more time I spend around her, it's only going to get worse.

"Fine. I'm going to Shade's room. This is bullshit," Ruby snaps as she climbs off the bed and heads for the door. I watch her walk out before I walk over and lock it. Bell looks up at me, a shine in her eyes as she licks her lips.

"You ready for me?"

"How can you want to do this after everything that's happened?"

"Look at you. You're fuckin' sexy as hell, and you're wearin' one of my t-shirts. I've been picturin' you in nothin' the whole goddamn day, Bell."

"This will never work," she says once more. I stalk toward her and pull the shirt off her body before I lean down and suck the flesh of her neck into my mouth.

"I'll make it work."

"That feels so good," she moans as I lick my way across her neck.

"Does that mean you're gonna be a good little girl?"

"Are you going to spank me if I'm not?"

"Baby, I'm gonna spank you anyway."

Chapter Fourteen

Annabell

Things with Ryan have been intense. He's intense. I wasn't sure that he would let me leave after the last few days of being with him. He seemed to have other things on his mind, but he kept me close by. Ruby has been a mess of her own making with Shade but today is the day we get to go home. I couldn't be happier because we've missed a few days of classes and now we have to make those up.

"What are you goin' to school for anyway?" Ryan asks as we walk up the steps toward the apartment.

"Nursing."

"You wanna be a nurse?"

"I like to help people."

"You can be my nurse any fuckin' day," he says through a laugh.

"You always have your mind on sex?"

"Most of the time I'm near you, I do. I can't help thinkin' about you bent over waitin' for me, baby."

"How is this going to work, Ryan? I don't know how to do this."

"Have you ever dated anyone before?" he asks me as we walk into the apartment.

"Yeah. Obviously."

"Same thing, only there is no one else but me, Bell."

"So we're dating?" I ask him, confused by what he's saying.

"You're mine. There is no one else."

"That really answers my question."

"What else is there to say? You are mine, Bell. Datin'? If you want to call it that, that's fine by me. I don't give it a shit how you label us." His eyes are on fire as he looks at me, and it makes me squirm. How can this work? He's bad for me. He's bad for his sister, and I can't stop thinking about him. What the hell is wrong with me?

"I don't know what you're thinkin', but you need to stop. I'm not goin' anywhere even if you want me to."

"That's real fair," I mumble. In seconds Ryan is across the room and grabbing my chin in his hand.

"Life isn't fair. Neither is this. If I say I'm keepin' you, then I'm keepin' you, Bell."

"You barely know me," I whisper. It's been years since we've talked to each other.

"I know enough. I might not have been talkin' to you all those years, but I know enough about you."

"You kept tabs on me?"

"You're Ruby's best friend. Of course, I kept tabs on you," he responds casually. I reach up and swat his hand away from my face before taking a step back.

"Get out, Ryan," he chuckles.

"Nice try."

"I mean it. Get out. This is all too weird, and I'm not comfortable," I tell him. This is all too much. He has known about me? Kept tabs on me? How weird is that?

"You think you run this relationship? You can't tell me what to do, Bell." He steps closer, and I retreat a step.

"I just did."

"And I didn't listen," he says, stepping even closer now. My back hits the wall as Ryan crowds my space. The door opens and closes when I hear Ruby.

"For fucks sake, can you two stop already?"

"I'm trying to!" I protest as Ryan stays in my space. His fingers curl around my chin, lifting my head so I'm looking up at him. His eyes are so intense that I don't know how to respond to him.

"Tell me you're mine, Bell," he whispers as he licks his lips. God, why does he have to be so damn perfect? What's even wrong with me to want a guy like him?

"I …"

"Say it." His demand runs through me like hot lava, and I find myself nodding my head as the words tumble from my lips.

"I'm yours." He grins and presses his lips to mine before pulling back and turning to face his sister.

"Someone will be here tomorrow to put in an alarm system. So don't give them any shit," he tells her.

"Oh no. I wouldn't dream of that," she responds sarcastically.

"I mean it, Ruby. Let them work and do their thing."

"Don't give them shit, darlin'," Shade adds.

"Whatever, alpha one and two."

"I mean it. I'll spank your ass," Shade tells her, making me laugh.

"Laugh it up, Bell. My brother will do the same to you," she says with a grin.

"This is getting out of hand now. Can we just be left alone now?"

"Thought we'd order pizza," Shade chimes in once more. I let out a sigh as he and Ryan pull out their phones and drop onto the couch. Ruby motions for me to go into the bedroom, and I happily do.

"What the hell, Ruby?"

"It's like they've taken over our lives in a matter of days. What the hell is wrong with them?"

"Can you say alpha male at its finest?"

"What did Ryan say?" Ruby asks, and I give her the breakdown of the conversation about how I have no say in when and where he shows up.

"This is insane. We should just go out there and tell them to fuck right off. We don't need them. We're capable of handling our lives all on our own," she says, holding her head high.

"Yes, we are!"

"But did you see how cute Shade is?" she whines.

"He is pretty hot."

"You can't say that. You're screwing my brother."

"He's still hot," I tell her with a smile.

"He is, right? So how do we make the hot guy leave?"

"Tell him you're on your period."

"Yeah, I don't think he cares."

"Tell him you're tired. We have class tomorrow," I remind her.

"You think that's going to stop them?" she asks.

"Okay. So we're stuck with them tonight."

"Don't sound so sad, Annabell." I don't miss the sarcasm.

"Well! What am I supposed to do?"

"Kick my brother out?"

"Like he'd go." Just as I'm about to say more, the door flies open, and Ryan walks in.

"What the hell are you two doin'?"

"I could have been naked, Ryan!" Ruby snaps at him.

"But you're not. What are you doin'? Plottin' ways to make us leave?" How the hell did he know that?

"No."

"Yes." Ruby and I say at the same time.

"We're not leavin' tonight, so nice try. Pizza will be here in a few minutes. Then you two need to go to sleep."

"I'm just about sick of you telling me when my bedtime is, Ryan," Ruby snaps at him.

"You have class in the mornin'."

"And? That doesn't mean I need you to tell me to go to bed," she adds.

"Stop bein' so damn stubborn. I doubt you'll be sleepin' much tonight anyway," he chuckles.

"Yes, I will. He's sleeping on the couch next to you."

"Like fuck I am."

"Ryan! You can't just keep that girl all to yourself."

"Yeah, I kinda can. She's mine, Ruby. Get used to it."

"Do you two always argue like this? I don't remember this from years ago," I ask.

"Oh, she's always this fuckin' mouthy," Ryan tells me.

"And you've never been this bossy. I don't like it. I'll kidnap Bell. I'll hide her ass," Ruby says, making me giggle.

"You think she's funny? Do you have any idea what I'd do to this town if you were taken?" His tone has turned serious as he eyes me. Ryan's eyes are darker than I've ever seen them.

"I'm not going anywhere," I remind him.

"Goddamn right, you're not."

"Pizza's here," Shade calls from the other room. Ryan turns and walks out, leaving Ruby and me to ourselves.

"That was intense."

"No shit," she says.

"You think he's always going to be like this?" I ask her.

"I don't know. I don't know what his deal is, to be honest. He likes you that much is obvious."

"Yeah, but he's so bossy. I don't know if I can handle some guy talking to me like that all the time." Admitting that felt good. I couldn't say it to Ryan, so I told Ruby.

"I don't know either. I think you two are going to butt heads at some point."

"I agree. I've been pretty compliant with him, but I don't know how long that's going to last," I tell Ruby.

"Let's go eat. Then we can figure out how to kick the guys out. I think we need some girl time anyway."

"Yes!   We   do."

Chapter Fifteen

Cowboy

Days have turned into weeks. Weeks of Bell in my head. I can't get her out, and I don't know that I want to. I've been with her every spare second, and it's still not enough.

"Cowboy, where's your head at?"

"On his girl," Shade answers for me.

"Fuck off. You've been bangin' my sister. I should beat your ass for that."

"Why? I'm keepin' her busy and off your ass," he laughs.

"You're probably right," I add.

"We haven't heard a word out of Howlers MC. I'm worried," Tyrant says, pulling all of our attention to him at the head of the table.

"What are you thinkin'?"

"Fuck if I know, brother. The traffickin' shit is hittin' close to home too. I don't like not knowing what the fuck is going on or who is involved. I want ears on the streets," he orders, looking at all of us. I nod my head agreeing with him on that. We need to know what's going on in our city.

"What do we have on the traffickers?" Maverick asks as he brings his beer to his lips.

"Not a lot. They're local. We know that much."

"We'll feel it out. Find out where they are," I say.

"That would be the easy way, yeah, but we don't know if they're stayin' local. They could just be sendin' someone in from out of the city to pick up girls."

"That's fucked," Shade curses under his breath.

"Beyond fucked. We think they're comin' up out of Atlanta to grab and go. The numbers of illegals are high here, as we all know. Missin' girls aren't often reported," Ty explains.

"So, what's the plan?"

"We feel it out this week. We make our presence known. We want them to see us and know we're out there lookin'."

"Isn't that gonna bring more heat on the club?"

"Maybe. Maybe not. Either way, I want it done. This club can handle a lot of shit. We can take it." The guys all nod their heads, grabbing their beers from the table in front of them. I light up a cigarette.

"So we make our presence known, and then what? Take out who we need to?" Shade asks.

"That's the plan. You see anything, hear anything that doesn't sit right with you, you move on it. We don't need to vote on that shit. These motherfuckers don't need to be in our city. They're stealin' our kids, our females. That's wrong, and we'll stop it."

Ty's annoyance and attitude are warranted. I agree with him one hundred percent. You can't have this kind of shit in your city. We have to clean it up.

"I'm all on board for this."

"Good. We don't need a vote. This is what it is. We're doin' this," he says. I nod and take a long drag off my cigarette before blowing smoke into the air.

"You think Howlers MC has anything to do with the traffickin'?"

"I don't know. I wouldn't suspect their MC, but you can't put shit past them. I didn't think they had the balls to shoot at our clubhouse either. I was wrong there. Speakin' of, we need to vote on what to do next. Either we sit this one out and see what happens, or we can go at them full force."

"I vote full force. They came at us, at our families," I add. I'm still pissed about that hole in the wall that could easily have taken out Ruby or Bell. I'm pissed they had to endure that.

"Let's vote." Tyrant goes around the table as each person in the room gives their vote. Of course, I'm all in for this shit. I want those motherfuckers dead. I want every one of them who hurt my girl. I want to see them bleed.

"That's that. We move on them first. We'll set it up and play it out. Movin' on their clubhouse as they did ours." The guys grunt their agreement. Ty slams the gavel down, ending church as I shove out of the chair and head for the door. I don't make it far when I hear her voice. What the hell are they doing here now?

Pushing through the door, I see her standing there next to one of the prospects. Her eyes meet mine, a smile curling her lips. I stalk toward her, stopping when I'm crowding her space.

"What are you doin' here?"

"Came to see you. Ruby had a late class," she says.

"What did I tell you about goin' out alone?"

"You told me not to, but Ruby was busy," she tries to justify what she's done. It's cute.

"You don't listen," I tell her.

"I was bored."

"And? That means you go out by yourself?"

"I called you twice and texted." I walk back over to the basket and grab my phone out.

"I was in church."

"And that's my fault?"

"Why are you here?" I know there's a reason she just showed up.

"I was just … fuck I wanted to make sure you were alone." Her admission shocks me a little. I wasn't expecting that. Grabbing her chin roughly in my hand, I force her to look up at me.

"You came here to see if I was fuckin' someone else?" She averts her eyes, so I squeeze harder, forcing her gaze back to mine.

"It's just … I …"

"You what? Tell me the fuckin' truth, Bell."

"Yes, okay? I mean, shit, Ryan. I see the girls around here."

"Are you fuckin' kiddin' me right now? They are club whores, Bell. You're you."

"What's that mean?"

"That means you're mine. Jesus, how many times do I have to say it?"

"I don't know!" she yells right before I drag her face to mine. I kiss her as I've never kissed her before. I run my hand under her shirt, grabbing her tit in my hand, flicking my thumb over her nipple. She moans into my mouth as I walk her backward toward the couch.

"You're about to learn a lesson," I warn her ahead of time. My lips keep claiming her, licking and sucking at her flesh. I don't care that everyone can see. I don't care that I'm leaving my marks all over her. I want her marked. I want her to wake up tomorrow and see what I did to her.

When her legs hit the couch, I lay her down and hike her skirt up. I growl when I find she isn't wearing any panties.

"You walked around like this?" I ask her, finding her wet and ready for me. I run my fingers through the wetness and groan when I find her clit. I circle it slowly as I lick my way down her neck.

"Everyone can see us," she whispers as I pull my hand away and undo my jeans. I pull my cock free and rub it through her wetness.

"Fuck, Bell. So goddamn wet."

"You need to stop. They're watching us," she's whispering now.

"This is what you get. This is your punishment for thinkin' I'm fuckin' someone else." I slam into her. Her cries could be heard through the clubhouse as I fuck her on the couch.

I pull back and lift her leg over my shoulder so I can get deeper inside her. I roll my hips, hitting her in all the right ways. She grabs my arms, holding on while I ride her hard.

"Goddamn," I hear Maverick roar, but I ignore his ass and focus on her, on my Bell. I lean down and kiss her again just as I see her lips part and words forming on her tongue. She wanted this. She deserves this.

"Ryan," she moans my name.

"You wanna come? Is that what you're beggin' me for?" I ask, slipping my hand in between us to find her clit. I work her clit in soft circles before I feel her tense up around me. I thrust harder, feeling her clench before she comes in a wave of pleasure. I follow behind her, letting my release hit me harder than I thought it would.

I pull out of her and adjust her skirt before pulling her to her feet. I know my cum drips down her thighs, and that's all on her. She should have thought about that beforehand.

"I can't believe you just did that," she sounds angry.

"You're serious right now? You came in here with that bullshit in your head, and you can't believe I'd fuck you in front of everyone?" I ask her.

"They saw everything, Ryan!"

"Yeah, we did," Mav chimes in. I flip him off as Bell spins on her heel and heads for the door. I don't let her get that far before I'm grabbing her arm and pulling her back.

"Ask any of them. Go ahead."

"Like they wouldn't lie for you," she hisses at me.

"I'm claimin' your ass in front of everyone. She's mine!" I bellow loud enough the whole club can hear me. There's applause and cheers, but I see the look on Bell's face. She doesn't understand.

"And that means what?"

"It means you're his. He'll protect you from now on. Cowboy will take care of you. You belong to him and only him." Tyrant explains it to her. Bell stares at me, unsure what to say. "He ain't been with the girls here." He adds.

"This is insane," she mumbles, making me grin.

"It is what it is. Don't fuckin' question me again, Bell. I haven't been with any of the girls here, and I don't plan on it."

"What if you change your mind?" she asks, all innocent-like. Look at her. Such a fucking beautiful girl, and she doesn't even realize it.

"I won't. Come on."

Chapter Sixteen

Annabell

After being fucked a few more times, he finally let me leave. I don't know what I was thinking going there either. I was just so insecure about everything, but now I know my place.

"You look happy," Ruby declares as we walk down the road.

"I am happy. Shouldn't I be?" I ask, glancing over at her.

"Of course you should be. I want you to be happy, Bell."

"I want you to be happy too."

"I am. I'm just tired from school and everything."

"I am too. It's exhausting. I never thought it would be this hard," I confess.

"Me either, but we're doing a good thing, right?" I nod my head because we are. We're making something out of our lives.

We walk a little further when a van pulls up next to us. I ignore it and keep going, but men jump out and grab us from behind before we get too far. I try to fight him off, but it does no good. Before I know what's happening, I'm being thrust into the back of the van with Ruby next to me. As soon as they have us inside, the van takes off. Fear spikes in my stomach, causing it to roll. Is it them again? Is it the same ones who shot at the clubhouse?

"Isn't this a surprise? Lookin' for one girl and got two," a man states as Ruby and I huddle together.

"What do you want with us?" I ask, my voice shaking.

"Don't you worry. You'll find out soon enough." I try to huddle closer to Ruby, keeping my arms around her trembling body. I don't make eye contact with the guy, but I look him over, trying to see if he's wearing a cut like the others were. I don't see one, but it is dark in the back of this van.

"Please. Just let us go," Ruby begs as the man laughs.

"Can't do that. I need you too much." Bile rises in my throat as I keep my grip on Ruby.

The ride in the van doesn't take long. Once the van stops, we're blindfolded and ushered out of the back. The cool air hits my skin, and I shiver as we're lead into a building.

"Where do you want them?" The man with his hand on my shoulder asks.

"Back room," someone tells him. It's them. I recognize the voice. It's one of the guys from the other clubhouse. What could they want with us?

I'm shoved forward, causing me to stumble before righting myself. I keep walking until I hear a door open, and I'm pushed inside. When I hear the door close, I reach up and pull my blindfold off at the same time Ruby does.

"It's them. What are we going to do?"

"They took my cell," she whispers.

"They didn't check me." That's when it hits me. We could call the cops. We can call for help. I slide my phone out as I watch the door before looking at Ruby.

"Call Ryan."

"What? No. I'm calling the cops!" Ruby shakes her head, and I'm confused.

"They can't help us. Ryan can. His club can. Just call him," she repeats. I dial Ryan's number and listen as it rings, praying to God he answers.

"Hey."

"They took us. Those guys took us," I tell him quickly when I hear footsteps.

"What? Slow down. What guys?"

"Ryan! Fuck, they're coming back. The same guys from the other clubhouse."

"Little bitch," the guy yells before grabbing my phone from my hand and backhanding me across the face.

"Ryan!" Ruby and I both scream at the same time when I'm hit again. My head spins as I fall on my ass from the blow. He doesn't come after me again, just brings the phone to his ear. I can hear Ryan yelling and cursing on the other end.

"I'll fuckin' kill you!"

The man starts to laugh.

"Not if I kill them first." Then he hangs up the phone and walks out of the room. Ruby drops down next to me, cupping my face in her hand.

"Are you okay?"

"I'm a little dizzy, is all."

"Ryan will get us out of this."

"What if he can't? We don't even know where we are," I sob as tears spring to my eyes. They fall down my cheeks, and Ruby's tears begin too. We cry, holding onto each other.

"It'll be okay. It has to be okay."

"I'm scared, Ruby."

"Me too, but Ryan heard you. You heard him, right? He's pissed. He'll find us." The door opens, and another man walks in, glaring at us. He looks us over before a sick grin crosses his face. He doesn't say a word or make a move, just walks back out of the room. I recognize him as the one I was dancing with.

"It was him."

"The one you were dancing with," she says softly.

"What do you think they want?"

"I don't know, Bell. I don't know what they want."

We sit huddled together, and a million things run through my mind. We shouldn't have been out there. We should have been at home. Ryan warned us about being out on our own, but we were together. I thought we'd be fine. I don't know what they could possibly want with us unless they know we've been at Ryan's clubhouse. Maybe they followed us there? Maybe they think we're rivals of theirs? I don't know what to think, but my heart pounds in my chest like it's going to jump out of me, and I can't stop shaking. This is a mess. What if Ryan doesn't get to us? What if he can't find us?

"Whatever bad you're thinking, stop. Ryan will find us."

"We don't even know where we are, Ruby." Tears roll down my cheeks as I think of all the bad stuff that could happen to us. Last time, she got out unharmed, but will it be the same this time? I don't want anything bad to happen to Ruby.

"It's okay. Ryan is smart, Bell. He'll find us."

"I hope you're right." She pulls me into her arms, both of us a sobbing mess. I don't know what to do with myself, but I do know we need to find a way out of here. We have to get out of this place.

"We need to find a way out," Ruby says what I've been thinking. The room is dark, but there's a little light peeking in from what appears to be a window. I nod toward it, and we both move. I run my fingers along the edge to find a windowsill, but when I try to shove it open, it won't budge.

"It's stuck."

"Then we break it. There has to be something in here we can use." Ruby turns and begins to feel her way through the room. I do the same, but I don't feel anything except a mattress on the floor. There's nothing in here. No chair, no lamp. Nothing. Hope deflates in my chest as I realize we're trapped.

Chapter Seventeen

Cowboy

"Calm the fuck down, Cowboy. I mean it," Tyrant warns me as I break another bottle. I'm pissed, beyond pissed. They have the girls. They shouldn't have been out alone, and now they have them.

"You can't tell me to calm down! They have my sister and my girl, Ty! Doing fuck knows what to them right now!" I know this isn't his fault, but I can't help but feel pissed at everyone. Fury courses through my veins right now, and all I want is blood.

"We're gonna get them back," he tells me.

"I know we are. I'm gonna kill every single one of those motherfuckers, and if they hurt either of them …" I let that sentence linger in the air. I'll make them all suffer. I will draw out their deaths until there is nothing left of them, and then I'll do it all over again. They don't know me. Not the real me.

"We need a plan," Mav announces as I shake my head.

"We have a plan. We go in there guns blazin' and kill those motherfuckers!"

"As much as I'd like to do that, we can't risk the girls bein' in there when we fire, Cowboy." Shade, the voice of reason. I don't know why he's so damn calm about all this. Why isn't he angrier than he is right now? Unless he doesn't feel shit toward my sister. That thought pisses me off further.

"You serious right now?" I turn on him. His hands are up, trying to ward off the impending ass beating he's about to get. We should go in there guns hot. Killing every Howlers MC member, we can fucking get our hands on. I want them all dead by the time this is over.

"We can't just go in there killin' them all. What if they're holdin' the girls someplace else? How are we gonna find them?" Maverick adds. It makes sense but not in my fucked up head. In my head, I just want them all dead, and I don't care how that has to happen.

"Fine. We don't kill 'em all, but we kill most."

"You're out for blood today," Tyrant adds. No shit. They stole what doesn't belong to them. Of course, I want blood.

"We need to move soon. They could be movin' them around."

"I agree. Let's head out. We have everyone on standby and ready." Ty finally says the words I've been waiting for. I'm thankful he took it seriously when Bell called me, and I'm fucking grateful he called backup in right away too. Our club isn't huge, but we have other MC's we trust locally who will have our backs. Hell, if we had more time, we have another chapter south of here, but we don't have that kind of time on our hands. They could be doing anything to those girls.

"Let's move out," Tyrant calls out to everyone. I light a cigarette, trying to calm my nerves as we head out the door. I blow smoke into the sky and watch as it curls and disappears. They have to be okay, both of them. I couldn't live with myself if something happened to either one of those girls.

"Get your head right before we even leave this parkin' lot, Cowboy. You can't be in there fuckin' up." Mav warns. I nod my head, rubbing the back of my neck before flicking the cigarette to the ground.

"I'm ready, brother. Been ready since she called."

"Heard that, but you need to stay calm. Shit's about to take a turn when we hit that clubhouse." I nod my head, knowing all that. This isn't our first time hitting a clubhouse before, but it is the first time we've had someone taken. We don't know what we're up against. We have no idea what we're fighting. Yet we're ready. We're ready for whatever they throw our way. This wasn't the plan. We were supposed to make a plan to handle them. We wanted to retaliate, but not like this. It was supposed to be organized and a straight shot. Now we're forced to go in when we aren't quite ready, which could get us killed. It could get the girls killed.

"Let's roll," Ty calls out as I climb on my bike and pull my helmet on. I rev the engine and follow the guys out of the parking lot. Adrenaline is running wild in my veins right now.

The ride to their clubhouse is thick with tension. I can feel how tight my muscles are coiled. I try to relax, but this is my sister's and my girl's life on the line.

We park the bikes and kill the engines before climbing off when we get as close as possible without them seeing us. We're going to have to go in the rest of the way on foot.

"Half around back, half around front. If they ain't wearin' a cut, don't shoot. Watch for the girls. Call out if you find them," Tyrant orders. Everyone nods their agreement before we split into groups and head toward the clubhouse. We use the trees as our cover and stalk toward the building.

When we're close enough, half move around back while others move to the front. I'm at the front of the line, ready to kick the fucking door in when it opens, and one guy walks out. I raise my gun and fire, watching him fall to the ground before more begin to move out. Just like that, we all start firing as we move in closer.

"Move in!" Tyrant roars. We move in, walking through the front doors as the others move in the back.

"Get on the fuckin' ground!" I order as I aim at the people inside. A few girls linger, dropping to the floor quickly. The guys look as though they want to challenge us, and that's fine with me too. I'll gladly kill every one of them. But when they see the number of us moving in, they drop their weapons and fall to the floor.

"Where's your Prez?" I call out, waiting for someone to answer me. No one does, and that pisses me off. I aim the gun at one of the guys on the floor and pull the trigger. "I'll ask once more! Where is your prez?"

"He ain't here," one of the guys finally answers me. I glance at Tyrant as he looks around the room.

"Where is he? Where are the girls?"

"What girls?" One asks. I decide it'll be him I use as bait for the others. I bend down and rip the asshole up from the floor to see the VP patch on his chest.

"Look what I found," I say to Tyrant. He walks over and takes a look at the patches before eyeing the guy.

"Where's the fuckin' girls you stole?" The guy opens his mouth, but Ty shoves his gun in before he can speak. "Don't make me ask twice."

"They aren't here," he mumbles around the barrel that's half down his throat.

"Where the fuck are they?" I ask this time.

"Safe house," he replies as he looks between Ty and me.

"Tie him up. He's gonna be our little bargainin' chip." I smirk at Ty before pulling the handcuffs and piece of rope from my back pocket. I knew we were going to have to play with some of them, so I came prepared. I cuff his wrists behind his back before tying his legs together as well. Then I shove his ass back onto the floor while we sweep the rest of the clubhouse.

When we come up empty, Maverick and Shade start pulling the trigger. Each man lying on the floor gets a bullet in the back of the head. The girls are set free and told to keep their mouths shut or end up as their friends did. You can tell by the look in their eyes they weren't going to say a word.

"Bring this motherfucker with us. Or we can torture him right here," Ty says, causing me to grin.

"Why not let him see his dead boys a little longer?"

"Fuck you!" The man, Vortex, spits. At least that's what his cut says. I kneel, pulling my knife free from its sheath as I look at him. Then I place the tip against his cheek and slice. Blood rushes to the open cut and runs down his cheek as he grits his teeth.

"Fuck you? That's the best you can come up with right now? I want the girls. Tell me where they are, and I make this painless."

"I told you at a safe house."

"Where?" he chuckles as he stares me dead in the eye. I know he isn't going to tell me. We're going to have to track these motherfuckers down. My heart sinks a little in my chest as the thought hits me hard. They could hurt them in the time it takes us to find them.

"Where is it?" I roar this time, but the bastard only laughs. At the end of my rope, I drag the blade across his throat and watch as he sputters for air. His body falls back onto the floor as strange sounds leave his lips.

"He wasn't gonna talk anyway," Shade adds.

"I know."

"Now what?"

"Now we set up shop. We stake out anywhere and everywhere they could be. They have to step outside at some point, and someone will see them."

"We put out feelers, and when someone has somethin', we move on it," Tyrant says.

"I don't like this. They could be hurtin' them."

"That's a given, Cowboy, and you need to be ready for that." I don't like hearing it, but I know it's true. They'll torture them, and if they're involved with the trafficking shit, god only knows how much time they have left.

"We need to do this quickly," I tell them. Shade's on his phone already making calls as Ty pulls his out to do the same. I walk past the bodies on the floor and step outside into the cool air. Pulling a cigarette from the pack, I light it up to try and calm my nerves, if only a little.

"I'm gonna find you two."

Chapter Eighteen

Annabell

Ruby sobs in the corner as the pain shoots through my body. I don't know how long I've been hanging here being beaten and tortured. We haven't eaten or been given anything to drink. My head feels like it's been put into a blender. I'm dizzy and sick to my stomach, but I can't move. My arms are bound above my head, chained to the ceiling. My legs ache, and I'm sure Ruby feels much the same. After we attempted to escape, they tied us up. We didn't make it far. We tried; God did we try.

"Ruby?" She doesn't answer, and that makes me nervous. No one has told us what they wanted with us. No one has said a word. They just keep us hanging here, coming in occasionally to beat on us.

"Ruby?" I call her name again.

"I'm okay," she whispers in the darkness of the room. She's not okay. I've tried to pull their attention away from her, and for the most part, I was successful.

The door creaks open, and I know it's time for another round. A man walks in with a knife in his hand. I know this is going to be bad. It's going to be worse than the last round.

"You still bein' a bitch?" he asks through a snarl.

"Are you still disgusting?" I hiss in his direction. He moves closer, pressing the tip of the blade to my stomach before I feel the pinch of the blade as he presses into my flesh. I wince but I bite the inside of my mouth to keep from crying out from the pain.

"You're not the smartest one here. Your friend is," he tells me as he drags the blade through my flesh. "We thought about sellin' you, but where's the fun in that? I like the idea of playin' with my toys." I internally cringe at his words.

"Fuck you," I snap. He just chuckles and digs the knife in deeper. Tears spring to my eyes as he continues his torture. Finally, when I sob, he pulls away and backhands me across the face. The sting isn't any worse than the pain in my stomach right now.

"You better get used to this."

"What do you want from us?" Ruby finally screams.

"What do we want? We don't want nothin' from you. We want what your boys have, and as soon as we can take them out, we'll have it." His words sting. This is because we were with Ryan and his club. At first, I thought it was random, but now I know. That doesn't change how I feel about Ryan; it just confuses me more. I wait until the asshole leaves the room before talking to Ruby.

"He'll find us."

"He has to, right?" she sobs.

"He will. I know he will. He loves you, Ruby," I remind her. She sobs harder and I wish I could hold her. I wish I could wrap my arms around her and keep her close to me, but I can't.

I try not to focus on the blood dripping down my stomach, but the warmth is there. The pain is intense as I shift to try and get a little bit of comfort. It does no good. Instead, I let my head drop forward, and my eyes fall shut.

This is hell. If hell were a place, this would be it. My head is spinning as I try to keep my balance. My legs are weak, and I'd probably hit the floor if my arms were released.

"Did you hear that?" Ruby asks. I lift my head and try to make out any sounds she might have heard, but I don't hear anything. I think she's becoming delusional.

"I don't hear anything."

"There!" she yells when we both hear a popping sound. It sounds like gunshots. God, please don't let one of the stray bullets hit me.

"Probably another club. They seem to have a lot of rivals." I'm weak. Too weak to keep my head up, so I let it drop back down when we hear more pops. Each one sounds closer than the last. My nerves are firing off until the door opens, and I slowly lift my head.

"Fuck!" Maverick roars, "In here!" They found us. They finally found us. Tears roll down my cheeks as the room fills with guys, but it's Ryan who guts me. His eyes are torn between Ruby and me, but I nod at him, letting him know his sister needs him now.

"I'm gonna find somethin' to cut this with," Maverick says. I nod my head and wait as Shade presses a piece of a rag to my stomach. I hiss and cringe, but I know he's just trying to stop the bleeding.

"I know it hurts, darlin'. But, we're gonna get you taken care of."

"Go to Ruby."

"Cowboy has her."

"She needs you too."

"You need me right now," he argues, causing the tears to fall harder.

"Please just go to Ruby." With a final plea, he nods his head and turns to walk toward her. I hear her cry harder when he gets to her. A few minutes later and Maverick is back, cutting me from the binds that held me up.

Like I thought, my legs are weak. I nearly fall to the floor when Tyrant scoops me into his arms.

"You're gonna be okay," he says.

"They want your club. They want everything."

"They're dead. All of them." I nod my head before resting it on his chest. I hear the growl, and I don't need to see to know it's Ryan. I want to go to him, I do, but I know Ruby needs her brother more than I do right now.

I let Tyrant carry me out of the house, looking over the bodies that litter the floor. My stomach turns, but there's nothing in me. We haven't eaten in days.

I'm placed in the back of a van before Ruby is placed next to me. Ryan climbs in and sits between us, wrapping an arm around each of us and pulling us in close.

"I'm so fuckin' sorry."

"It's not your fault."

"If I had kept you away," he shakes his head.

"We're alive," Ruby reminds him.

"Doesn't matter. Look what they've done to you." I can hear the anger in his tone. I can feel it vibrating off him. So I snuggle closer, let him feel me, and it allows me to absorb his warmth.

"You're in a bad way," he whispers into the top of my hair.

"I'll live."

"I'm sorry, Bell."

"Stop saying sorry. It wasn't your fault. We shouldn't have been out. You warned us."

"That doesn't matter. You should be able to walk the streets. Fuck!" Ryan shouts, causing me to jerk a little. He tightens his hold on me.

"What do you wanna do about this?" he asks Tyrant as he sits across from us.

"I'm callin' in the Royal Bastards from Savannah. Demon and Drake deal with a lot of this traffickin' shit. They might have some good insight."

"Wait. They're traffickers?" I ask.

"Yeah. I'm sure you wouldn't have been around much longer if we didn't get word on where you were," Tyrant explains, and my insides tremble.

"They were going to sell us?"

"Or trade you," Ryan adds. I grab my stomach feeling the warm crimson liquid still leaking out of my body. My head is spinning before I slowly close my eyes and rest my head on Ryan's shoulder.

When I wake up, I'm being carried into the clubhouse. It's a strange feeling having Ryan carrying me like this. I feel strange and wonder just how much blood I've lost.

I'm placed on a bed before another man comes over to me and starts checking me. I'm about to tell him to fuck off when Ryan tells me it's the doctor. I nod and let the man do his thing, although I don't feel much like letting anyone touch me.

Ruby looks traumatized as another man checks her over. Her eyes are wild, and I can't place the look in them.

"Is she okay?"

"She's in shock. She'll be fine. We're giving her some meds to help." I nod my head when I feel the prick in my stomach. I glance down and see he's numbing the area where I'd been cut.

"You need stitches. I'm numbing you up first, but this should heal just fine." I nod my head even though it hurts to do so.

Then I just close my eyes and let everything slowly slip away. I let the medicine he's injected me with do its job and take away the pain. I welcome the darkness that waits for me on the other side. I embrace it and let it pull me under.

Chapter Nineteen

Cowboy

Doc's kept the girls drugged for the most part. That's probably a good thing because they've both woken up screaming in their sleep. The nightmares they have are killing me, and they're both in my room. I do my best to give them both the attention they need right now, but it's hard. Shade has tried to stay with Ruby as much as possible so that I can look after Bell.

It's a mess. It's all a mess. Tyrant called in the Royal Bastards to help with the trafficking shit. Drake volunteered to come up here and see what he could do. He's on his way now. That doesn't mean this is over. It's just beginning. We need to find out who's in charge of all this shit and then handle them. It will never end, and we all know that, but at least we can stop what we can from here.

Bell stirs as I lean over and press my lips to the top of her head. I know she's had a rough time the last few days. She'd lost a lot of blood and was weak when we found her. Doc said any longer, and she probably wouldn't have made it. That's the part that makes me sick to my stomach. I could have lost her before I ever got the chance to love her. The reality of my thoughts hit me hard. Do I care enough about her to love her? I don't know the answer to that.

"How's she doin'?" Shade asks as he walks into the room with drinks and food. I haven't eaten in god, only knows how long. I've been too wrapped up in these two. He passes me a plate of food, and I gladly accept.

"She's been stirrin' a lot in her sleep."

"Doc said the meds shouldn't wear off. He's got them pretty doped up," he reminds me. I nod my head and take a bite of my food.

"Yeah. She hasn't woken up yet." I'm thankful for that too. She needs the rest. They both do, although it looks like Bell got the worse end of things.

"Ryan?" I hear Ruby call from the other side of the room. I had Tyrant move another bed into my room to be closer to the two of them. I rise from Bell's bed and walk over to Ruby, gently sitting on the edge.

"Hey, darlin'. How you feelin'?"

"I don't know. Everything's all fuzzy."

"Yeah, Doc has you on some good meds. You shouldn't even be awake."

"Is she okay?"

"She's healin'. That's all you need to worry about right now. Gettin' better."

"She would take the hits for me. Bell would egg them on to keep them away from me," she confesses as tears stream down her cheeks.

"She's gonna be okay, Ruby. I promise."

"Are they all dead?" she asks, now she knows what we do.

"All of them. We've got guys comin' in to help out with the rest," I tell her. She nods her head, her eyes slowly fluttering closed again. I need her to rest. I need her to get better.

"She's too stubborn not to pull through this, Ryan."

"I know. That much I know."

"Eat and take a walk. I'll keep an eye on them." I start to shake my head when I realize it wasn't an offer but an order. I've been in this room for days watching over the two of them. Standing, I stretch my legs and walk to the door before taking one last look at the two of them. They are both sleeping peacefully.

When I step into the hallway, I take a deep breath and head for the stairs. Once I'm in the main room, I walk over to the bar and grab myself a beer. Tipping it back, I take a long pull when Tyrant strolls over, slapping a hand on my shoulder.

"Thought you were never comin' out of there," he chuckles.

"Didn't like leavin' them."

"Heard that, brother. They'll be fine. Doc said so."

"Will they? They've been beaten and abused, Ty. How do they get past that shit? They were kidnapped."

"I know that, but those two are strong and will heal from this. Drake's on his way up here now. It should take him about two or three hours to make it. Then we'll talk about what's going down next."

"You got a plan?"

"Not really. I just know we need to find the asshole responsible for this shit. I don't want it in our city."

"Me either. It's enough that those two were taken. We're lucky we got them back."

"Exactly. The more that go missin', the more we're lettin' them get away with. We can't keep doin' that."

"I hear you, brother. I don't want that either, but we're lookin' at somethin' bigger than us."

"And we'll handle it as such. I'm not turnin' my back on this, Cowboy. I won't let what happened to them go unpunished." I'm glad he sees things that way because I feel exactly the same. I won't let this shit rest until I know the motherfuckers responsible are dead. I want everyone's fucking head for this.

"Drake's ready for blood?" I ask with a grin on my face. I already know he is. That's what he lives for.

"Hell yeah, he is. You know how sick that motherfucker is. He doesn't take lightly to traffickin' after what happened when he was young. I don't blame him there either. That shit hits close to home for him." I nod my head and take another long pull of my beer before lighting up a cigarette and relaxing a little.

"Yeah, I heard about that. Glad he's in on this. He has intel we don't."

"Damn right he does. He's been huntin' motherfuckers all over the state and country."

"He's that involved?"

Ty nods his head. "Helps other chapters out when they need it. We're good with the Bastards, so he's more than willin' to come up here."

"That's a good thing, brother. A damn good thing."

"Keep your head right, Cowboy. We don't want any missteps in this. I know those are your girls up there, and there isn't much I can say to make that better but keep your focus."

I nod as I inhale the nicotine into my lungs.

"I'm doin' the best I can right now."

"I know you are. Grab somethin' for the girls to eat and go back to them. I'll let you know when Drake shows up."

"Thanks, Ty." He nods his head as I walk over and grab a few beers from the bar. Then I'm turning and heading back up the stairs to my room. When I step inside, Shade looks up from his spot next to Ruby.

"You good?"

"Yeah, Drake's on his way up here."

"No shit?"

"That's what Ty said. Said he's as pissed as we are and out for blood."

"I bet he is."

"Yeah, shit hits too close to home for his likin'. I can't say that I blame him now that I'm in the same situation."

"Heard that. Just know I got your back on this," he declares.

"Thanks, brother. Appreciate that." Shade nods his head before looking back at Ruby. That's when Bell stirs. I walk over and set my beers on the table next to the bed before sitting in the chair.

"Ryan?"

"I'm here, darlin'."

"What's going on?"

"You're okay. You just had a lot the doc needed to take care of. You lost a lot of blood," I tell her.

"Is it bad?"

"Nothin' you won't recover from. You want anything?"

"Will you hold my hand?" How could I tell her no, I can't? I scoot the chair closer to the side of the bed and grab her hand in mine. That's when I see the tears leaking down her cheeks.

"You hurtin'?" I ask her, seeing the tears.

"Is Ruby okay? I tried to keep them away from her. I tried, Ryan."

"I know you did. She's fine. You're both gonna be fine."

"How do you know that?"

"Because you're mine, Bell. That's how I know."

Chapter Twenty

Annabell

I feel a ton better today. I still hurt and ache but getting out of that bed was the best feeling in the world. Ryan hasn't left my side unless he has to, which he did a few times now that they have a few guys from the other club here. He told me they were here to help.

"This is bullshit," Ruby whines as we sit against the back wall of the main room.

"What is?"

"That we're being treated like babies. We can both walk now." She's been upset that not only Ryan but Shade too has been bossing her around lately. I can't say I blame them either. We're both pretty fucked up.

"We look like shit," I remind her, and she laughs.

"We do, don't we?"

"Badly. It's like our faces were put into a meat grinder. I'm surprised the guys haven't run the other way," I joke with her.

"Are you okay, though? They came at you harder, and I know why. I would say thank you, but it isn't enough, Bell. You did the unthinkable, and I love you more than you know."

"Let's not do this. It hurts to cry," I tell her.

"You're right. Everything hurts."

"Twenty-seven stitches is killer," I remind her.

"Fuck, that's a lot."

"At least it was a real doctor. That's a plus. It could have been your brother stitching me up," I giggle a little at the thought.

"Oh god. It wouldn't even be a straight line."

"What are you two talkin' about?" Speak of the devil, and he appears.

"You," Ruby tells him.

"Is it good things? Like how hot I am?" Ruby makes a gagging sound that makes me laugh before I wince and grab my stomach. Ryan is there in seconds, kneeling in front of me with concern written all over his face.

"You okay?"

"Stop babying her! She's fine," Ruby snaps.

"Is that what you two are talkin' about?" I nod my head.

"I can walk, Ryan. I'm okay. I don't need you hovering over me like you are."

"I just want to make sure you're okay," he says, sounding sincere. I hate that I feel this way, but I know he's hovering, and I need the space.

"I know you are, and I appreciate that, but you need to give me a little space." His eyes flash darker before he nods, running his hand through his hair. I watch him stand and cross the room, heading straight for the bar. Then I watch him take down a few shots before his eyes come back to meet mine briefly. One of the guys calls his name, and he turns to look at him.

"That was intense."

"I don't want to hurt him, Ruby, but damn it, I need to breathe a little," I admit to her.

"I get it. I feel the same way, but I think with those two, we aren't getting much space."

"He's going to have to give me space, or I'll lose it. It's hard having him close to me. I don't want him away, but I don't want him near either. I don't understand this feeling I have."

"It's okay, Bell. I get it. I do."

"Do you?" I feel the tears prick at the back of my eyes as I look away from her. She scoots a little closer and wraps her arm around my shoulders, pulling me gently into her.

"We went through hell. We were dealt a shitty hand, and now we have to recover from that. They weren't there. They don't get it. The fear, the anger. All of it. They don't get it, Bell." Tears slowly slide down my cheeks before I reach up and wipe them away. I see Ryan across the room eyeing me like he wants to come over but he doesn't. He shifts from foot to foot when Tyrant stands in the middle of the room.

"We got an announcement that involves everyone here. This is Drake. Some of you know him, and others don't. He's the VP of the Royal Bastards MC down in Savannah, working closely with human trafficking rings. He works to bring them down and make them pay. The shit that happened up here hit close to home. It hit one of our own members sister and old lady. We don't let that shit ride in our city." The guys all roar as the girls clap their hands.

"We're gonna take them down one motherfucker at a time. There's gonna be blowback. That means the club is going back on lockdown until further notice."

"The girls are gonna stock up on shit, so if there's anything you need, let one of them know soon," Maverick adds. Everyone either agrees out loud or grunts their agreement. I glance over at Ruby as Shade walks up to her. Then I pull my gaze back to Ryan's. He's still staring me down from across the room, but he hasn't made a move to come this way. I don't know if I should be grateful or not. I don't know what to feel right now. Instead of debating it, I stand slowly, grabbing my stomach as I go. Then I walk toward the steps when Tyrant stops me.

"Drake's good at what he does," he tries to assure me as I stand near the stairs.

"I'm glad."

"I know this is hard for you. I know this is all new to you too. You were thrown into a livin' hell, and now you're in another. Recovery is just hard. Your emotions are all over the place, and you can't see straight. I've been there, Bell. I know you need your space. I can see it in your eyes but don't shut him out completely. I don't think he can handle that," he says. I feel a pinch in my chest. I don't like feeling.

"I'm trying. I really am."

"I know you are, darlin'. Just don't forget he is too. This is new for him too. He ain't never had an old lady around here."

"I'll do better."

"It's not about doin' better. It's about gettin' better. That's all we want for you. The rest is on us. We'll handle everything else." I nod my head and turn, walking up the stairs. I can feel Ryan coming behind me. I don't say anything as I trail up the steps and down to his room. As soon as I'm inside, he closes the door behind us.

"I'm tryin' here," his voice is soft.

"I know you are, and I'm sorry."

"Don't be. What happened was rough. It took somethin' from you that you can never get back."

"I feel like I need space, but I want you close at the same time. My head feels like it's out of control. The tears won't stop falling. I hate how I feel inside. I hate the way I look right now." I know my face is still swollen and bruised. I hate looking in the mirror.

"You look beautiful, Bell. Just like always. Don't doubt that. The other shit will heal. It's your head I'm worried about."

"What about it?"

"This kind of shit can and will fuck a person up. I don't want to lose you."

"I don't want to lose you either. I need you, Ryan."

"I'm not goin' anywhere, sweetheart. You have me."

"Are you sure?" He nods his head, and my stomach does little flips.

"Yeah, baby. I'm sure." He walks over closer and leans down into my space, pressing his lips to mine.

"You're mine, Bell. I'm gonna make sure every asshole who had anything to do with this shit pays the price."

"I'm yours," I whisper.

Chapter Twenty-One

Cowboy

"Look alive, Cowboy," Tyrant breaks the spell I've been under. My mind is a complete wreck. I can't think straight, knowing she's pushing me away. I get it, though. I get why she's doing it, but that doesn't mean I have to like it. She needs space to work on her shit, and I'm going to give it to her.

"I'm good," I reply as Drake stands at the front of the room.

"What do we know?" he asks, looking around the table.

"We know that Gainesville is a goddamn traffickin' hot spot. We know it's one of the biggest in North Georgia."

"Facts. What else?"

"We know that George Malley is a leader of whatever the fuck this ring is. We got intel he was involved with Howlers MC. That means he's the leader in this area," Maverick offers more information.

"Right. And those are also facts. He's the fuckin' leader of this shit, which means he's the one we go after. We need to take out his line first. We need decoys, and I have a few of those. Once we take down his chain of command, he'll be useless. That's when we hit him," Drake says.

"Sounds too easy," Shade chimes in.

"It's not. His chain of command is long. He has a lot of assholes on the street scopin' out new girls. The decoy girls I have are all trained in this shit. They were a part of it once, and they wanted their revenge. I know because I trained them myself," Drake informs us. It's interesting to hear he did all this himself.

"So what, we send them out and wait?"

"That's exactly what we do. When the assholes pounce, we move. We take them out and continue until we have them all off at the street level."

"Then what? How do we move up the chain of command?" I ask.

"That's easy. When Malley's underbosses lose their street soldiers, they'll have to recruit more. We watch and wait, just like with the first set of guys. Then we move. Eventually, George is gonna know what the fuck is happenin' and show his face. He thinks he's untouchable."

"He's mine," I growl.

"I don't care whose he is as long as he's dead at the end of this shit," Drake says. The guys nod in agreement, as do I. I want his ass for what happened to the girls. I want his ass for what's still happening to other girls out there.

"We go out. Make our presence known. He's gonna be lookin' for a new MC to run shit. Maybe we give him an offer he can't refuse."

"What do you mean?" Mav asks.

"What if we offered to traffic the girls? That way, we're on the inside of this. We use your decoy girls," I suggest. Drake seems to think about that for a second while I light up a cigarette.

"That could work. I could have my girls out on the street, and you could pick them up," Drake offers.

"Will that work? Get their attention?" Tyrant asks now.

"I don't know. I'd think it would capture their attention when girls start goin' missin' off the streets they're used to runnin'." It could work. I could see them getting pissed about that. We would be in their territory messing with their girls. It could be a win-win.

"Then we do it. We move on them."

"I like that idea," Drake says with a sick smirk. I bet he does. I've heard the rumors about him. I know he's a killing machine who goes after anyone who has anything to do with trafficking humans.

"I'm in," I add.

"This goes to a vote," Ty speaks up. He goes around the table, and everyone agrees. I didn't figure anyone would turn their backs on an opportunity like this.

"Then it's settled. I'll call in my decoy girls, and we'll get this shit rollin'," Drake declares before sliding his phone from his pocket. Ty slams down the gavel, and we all stand and head for the door. I walk out, but I don't see Bell or Ruby. I assume they're still holed up in the room. So I walk over and take the stairs two at a time to tell them the news.

When I get into the room, I see Bell but not Ruby.

"Where's Ruby?"

"She's taking a nap in Shade's room. She wanted some space."

"And you? You want space?"

"I don't know what I want, Ryan."

"I have news. We're gonna use decoy girls to get to the assholes who did this shit to you," I tell her.

"What do you mean, decoy girls?"

"Girls who have been trained to fight. Girls who have been through this before," I explain to her. I don't like the idea of girls being used as decoys, but it makes the most sense. Especially if Drake has them trained the way he says he does.

"No. You can't do that."

"Why?"

"They're probably traumatized, Ryan! That shit was scary for us, and we weren't even sent away. How do those poor girls feel?" she snaps at me. I understand her concerns. I understand why she worries, but I trust Drake.

"Drake is smart. He wouldn't put them out there if he didn't think they were gonna handle it well."

"Even still. I don't like it."

"Well, it went to vote. They're goin' in. We're gonna be the ones to take them."

"I don't understand."

"We're gonna take them. Make it look like we're the one's runnin' shit now that Howlers is out of the picture. They're gonna need a new MC to handle that shit for them. And we're gonna be the ones to do it."

"That's …" She doesn't finish her sentence before dropping her gaze to the floor. Bell doesn't know what to say, and I can't blame her. This is all a huge mess, but this is the only way for us to get in where we need to be. I walk over and cup her cheek in my hand before she finally looks up at me.

"I know you don't like this, but the girls will be safe. We're not gonna hurt them. They'll come back here and return home."

"Are you sure? What if there's someone else out there? What if someone else takes them?"

"We're puttin' trackers on them. No one is gonna get far with them if they try. We're gonna be watchin' them all the time. I promise things will be okay." Bell licks her lips before nodding her head and leaning into me. It's the first time she's actually wanted to be around me, and I savor every second of it. I understand why she's been distant; it doesn't mean I like it.

"As long as they're safe," she whispers. I know she doesn't like the idea of anyone being hurt how she and Ruby were. I can't say I like the idea either, but I won't let that happen to those girls. We have a plan that should go off without a hitch.

"I know I said I'd give you space, but I can't do it. I can't stay away from you," I admit.

"I know."

"You do?" She nods her head before looking up at me.

"I just don't know how to feel right now, Ryan. I don't know what any of this is."

"This is us, Bell. This is me lovin' you. This is me bein' here for you. I'm not the best guy in the world. I'm not even the best guy for you, but I'm tryin' here. You gotta give me somethin'." I'll beg her for a chance if I have to. I just need to know that she's in this with me. I can't give her space; I need her too much. Over the last few days, I've realized just how much I need her. I'm calmer, saner when she's close to me. The ugliness that runs wild in me calms when she's close.

"You have me, Ryan. I'm just confused," she admits.

"I know you are. I know things are hard right now, but they're gonna get better. I'm gonna make them better, Bell. I promise."

"I know you will." With that, she pushes up on her toes and brushes her cracked and bruised lips over mine. Nothing else matters in this moment. Just her. Just this. Just us.

"Oh hell. Already?" I hear Ruby mutter as she walks into the room. Bell smiles, and it's genuine and perfect.

"No one told you to barge in here," I remind her.

"No one told you to maul my best friend, but that hasn't stopped you."

"I'm glad to see your smartass mouth is back to normal," I say, making her laugh.

"Me too. I've missed the snarky side of me."

"I bet you have. You givin' Shade hell?"

"What kind of sister would I be if I didn't?" Ruby laughs, causing Bell to laugh too.

"She is good at it," Bell tells me.

"Who do you think you're talkin' to? I've had to deal with that mouth of hers all my life."

"And you love this mouth. You can't get enough of it," Ruby adds.

"I'd sure as hell miss it if anything ever happened to you," I tell her truthfully. Bell pulls away as I turn toward Ruby and open my arms. In seconds she's throwing herself into me, hugging me.

"You know you can't get rid of me that easily," she whispers against my chest.

"I wouldn't want to, Ruby. I'm glad you're here."

"Just not with Shade," she teases.

"I'm dealin' with that. I think he's a good guy with a shit past like most of the guys here, but I think he'd do you right."

"I don't know if it's even that serious."

"He can't seem to stay away, so I think it's somethin'." She might not see it, but I do. There's something there. Shade is just a little more cautious than others. He's been burnt too many times, and that took a toll on him. He doesn't want to love someone or even care about them. Shade wants to fuck and walk away, but I see the look in his eyes when he sees my sister. It's different.

"Well, either way, I need some time to deal with everything that's happened. I don't know if I want to be a part of this life, Ryan. It's scary and dangerous."

"It is. That's what I signed up for."

"I didn't," Bell chimes in.

"Babe, you signed up the minute you were kissin' me. That was all I needed."

"I don't agree," she argues.

"You want out, Bell? You want to leave me? This is your only chance. If you don't walk out of this room right now, that's it; you're mine." I'm not trying to force her into staying, but she does have a choice to make. I'll be a good man and let her walk away for now if that's what she chooses to do but bet your ass I'll be back after her when this shit is over.

"Um, you're not moving," Ruby points out as she stares at her best friend.

"I don't think I can. As much as I hate what happened to us, I know Ryan would do anything he could to protect me from that ever happening again."

"Oh God, you're in love with him!" Ruby squeals.

"Shut up, Ruby," I tell her as I look at Bell. Does she love me? Is it possible after only this short amount of time?

"Are you Bell?" I ask. Her eyes find mine, and I can see all that I need to see in them. "Answer me."

"Yes."

Chapter Twenty-Two

Annabell

Saying I loved Ryan was easy. It came to me easily. Ruby had a million and one things to say about that, and I understand her concern. Unfortunately, this shit isn't over, and if I stay with Ryan, things will always be happening with the club. But I trust him. I trust him to keep me safe and out of harm's way. I trust he will do what's best for me.

"So, you love the man." Ruby makes me smile and will always be my best friend, but there's a place in my heart now for Ryan too.

"I can't help it."

"I get it, you know. He's cute, sweet when he wants to be. I think he's a good guy despite all this other shit. It's kinda my fault all this went down."

I shake my head. "No, Ruby. It isn't. We both decided to do what we did. I don't blame you for a second."

"You should. You should blame me. I was the one who thought it would be fun to go to that club. I should have known better. If Ryan didn't want me in this world, there was a reason, but I was stubborn as hell and didn't want to listen. I'm sorry, Bell. This was never what I wanted for you."

"Look what it's done, though. It's brought us closer together. It's brought me to Ryan. I think things happened for a reason, even as shitty as those reasons were. We're stronger now," I tell her. I think we are. I think we've grown since this happened. I would never do anything like that again.

"I hate that they happened, though. I hate that you had to go through that."

"I know, and I hate it for you too. But we're here. We're safe now. We can do whatever we want, be who we want. Nothing changes. We're still going to school and doing what we love."

"About that," she says, looking at her hands.

"What about it?"

"I don't know if I want to do it anymore. I mean, I saw what happened to you and I …"

"No. Don't do that. Don't you dare. You're a great nurse. You're a great student. We are going to finish what we started. Together." She looks up at me and nods her head. That's when Ryan walks back in.

"Shade is lookin' for you." Ruby nods her head before pulling me into a hug.

"I love you, Bell."

"I love you too." With that, she pulls away and heads for the door, punching Ryan in the arm on her way out. I smile and giggle a little when Ryan's eyes catch mine.

"What is it?"

"You're so fuckin' beautiful, Bell." My heart sinks in my chest, knowing there's still bruising on my face, yet he says those words to me. I walk over slowly and wrap my arms around his neck, pulling his lips to mine. I kiss him hard. I kiss him like he's the air I need to breathe. I kiss him as if I may never get the chance. Then he takes over. He kisses me the same way I'm kissing him.

"We gotta stop this, or I'm gonna lose it," he says, making me smile.

"I think I like you losing it."

"You have stitches."

"They're healing. I can move around a little better now," I tell him.

"Is that right?" I nod my head feeling the heat course through my body. I want him. I need him. I step back and pull the shirt over my head, tossing it to the floor before moving to my shorts next. They slide down easily when I kick them to the side. I stand in front of him naked as I had no bra or panties on, Ryan's eyes blaze.

"You're askin' for trouble."

"Am I?" I ask in a sultry tone. Ryan pulls his cut down his arms and tosses it onto the chair before peeling the rest of his clothes off. Then he's stalking toward me, gripping my face in his hands. His kiss is brutal and unforgiving, and I love every second of it.

"You gonna ride me, Bell?" he whispers against my lips. I nod, needing him inside me. He kisses me once more before climbing on the bed and laying on his back. Then he motions for me to come to him. Walking over, I climb on the bed carefully before straddling him. I'm careful with my stitches as I grab his cock and lower myself down his length. I don't know how hard I can go but feeling him filling me is the best feeling I've had in a long time. Slowly I rock my hips, careful not to hurt myself as his hands land on my thighs.

"Go slow if you need to." I nod and roll my hips until the pain starts to hit me. Then I slow down and ride him easily. It's not enough, but it's better than nothing. Ryan raises his hips, and it's like the world explodes around me. I love the feel of him inside of me. I love the feel of him touching me.

His hands roam up my legs and up my sides until he's pulling my nipples between his fingers. He tugs and twists making my stomach clench.

"Fuck," I hiss as the pain shoots through me, but I don't want him to stop. I need this.

"You wanna stop?" I shake my head. Hell no, I don't want to stop. I want him to come inside of me.

"Don't stop," I whisper as he raises his hips once more. I slowly ride him until I feel that warmth flooding through me. Then my orgasm hits, and everything, even the pain, seems to fade into the fog. Ryan isn't far behind me, exploding inside of me and hitting every piece of me. I let him finish before I carefully climb off and lay on the bed next to him. Ryan rolls to his side to look at me, brushing a piece of hair away from my face.

"You okay?"

"I'm fine. Just a little sore."

"We shouldn't have done that."

"I need that. I needed you," I tell him. A smile tugs across his face, lighting up the room.

"I did too. Tomorrow we send the girls out," he says as his fingers linger on my cheek.

"I hate this," I tell him.

"I know you do. I hate it too, but this is what we have to do. We need an in with that asshole, and this is the only thing he seems to care about. If there were another way, I'd do it, but this is it."

"I get it. I just don't like it."

"I know. The girls know what they're gettin' into, though. Drake told them."

"He's a little creepy."

"A little? Babe, he's a lot creepy. The shit he's done makes us look like boy scouts." I giggle a little, but I see the serious look in Ryan's eyes. I lean in and kiss him softly before pulling back and laying my head on the pillow.

"It'll be over soon?" I ask, praying to God that it's over soon. I don't want anyone else going through what we did or worse. And I know there are worse out there.

"It will. Then you'll be back in school and takin' care of me when I get busted up," he laughs.

"Oh, is that what you think? That I'll play naughty nurse for you?"

"Damn right. I want you in a slutty nurse costume doin' bad things to me." My cheeks heat at his words.

"You're crazy."

"When it comes to you, I am. I don't know what it is about you that makes me insane, Bell, but it's there."

"I feel the same way about you too. I hate when you're not near me."

"Well, it's a good thing I don't have to be away from you long then, yeah?"

"What do you mean?"

"I'm here, Bell. I ain't goin' anywhere."

"I know." I press myself closer to him and embrace   his   warmth.

Chapter Twenty-Three

Cowboy

"Cowboy, you seein' what I'm seein'?" Maverick asks over the walkie-talkie.

"Is that the man himself?" It's been a week. A week of us staging girls and picking them up. They're good, too, just like Drake said they would be. They fight us, and that's the beauty of all this. They make it look real.

"I think we attracted some attention," he replies.

"Looks that way. How do you wanna play this?"

"Callin' Drake now," he says, and I'm left with silence. I don't like the silence. I could easily run up on that asshole and take him out right now. I could end his worthless life in a matter of seconds. This could all be over, but who wants to do this the easy way? I sure as hell don't. I'd love to have him the shed back at the clubhouse.

I keep my eyes on him as he talks with another guy, eyeing a few of the girls who loiter close by. Luckily they are our girls and not just some girls off the street. Our girls know what to do if they get grabbed.

"Drake wants us to move on him. Stop at the girl's first, and when he makes a scene, take him."

"Got it."

"You ready, Shade?"

"Fuck yeah, I am."

"We move on three."

"One … two … three." As soon as the numbers leave Mav's mouth, we're on the move. I pull up in the van next to the girls when Tyrant hops out and grabs one. That catches George's attention, and he comes rushing over like he's about to save the day. Mav and Shade move in behind him, pressing guns into his back.

"Get in the van," Mav roars. George raises his hands and climbs in before the other two join us. The other girls climb in as well, and then there's a party in the back.

I switch places with the prospect who was riding shotgun with me and let him drive us back. I climb into the back with my gun drawn and ready to fire, but I know I can't. Instead, I slam the butt against the motherfuckers head and watch as the blood pours from the wound.

"Do you have any idea who the hell I am?" he growls.

"We know who you are. We know what you do, and that ends today," Tyrant snarls back.

"You can't just do this." His protests mean nothing. Mav moves in, checking him for guns, and pulls one from his waistband along with a knife and a cell phone from his pocket. Then he's behind him, zip-tying his hands together.

"What the hell is this?" he asks as we ignore him and drive.

"You'll see soon enough." Ty is trying to control his anger. I can see it from here, but he wants to get dirty just like the rest of us. He wants blood.

"This is bullshit. You want money? I have money!"

"Making money off poor girls just like we used to be?" One of the girls throws at him. They were supposed to remain silent, but it doesn't look like that's happening. Not that any of us would stop her if she killed the son of a bitch right now. She deserves that much.

"I don't even know you."

"Probably not. Do you really know any of the girls you steal and sell? Do you know their names? Their lives? I had a mother who was sick. Did you know that she died while I was being passed around by the men you sold me to?" Before he can respond, she spits in his face before sitting back against the side of the van. I place a hand on her shoulder and give her a soft nod. She smiles back at me. She needed to get that out, and I don't see the problem with that.

The closer we get to the clubhouse, anticipation runs through my veins. Do I let the girls see him? Do I let them see this is finally going to be over? Or do we just kill the motherfucker and be done with it? Could they handle seeing him killed? No, I don't think they could. They aren't that kind of girls.

We pull into the clubhouse parking area and head around back, out into the field where the shed is. When the prospect stops, we jump out, pulling the asshole along with us.

"Can I stay?" One girl asks me.

"Ty, you good with her stayin'?" I ask him. He looks at me and then at her before nodding his head.

"You're good, darlin'." She nods her thanks as we drag the asshole into the shed. This was all too easy. I was ready for a fight, but this will do too.

We're met by Drake and an array of tools set out on the table just inside. My heart leaps when I realize he's going to torture the asshole.

"What's all this?" I ask, nodding toward them as Mav and Ty tie Malley to the chair in the center of the shed.

"Toys."

"Toys?" He smirks. A dark deadly smirk that makes my stomach turn. He's as crazy as they said he was.

"I like to play with them a little." I nod my head as I turn to see Malley squirming in the chair.

"I can pay you! I can pay all of you!"

"No one wants your money. We want your life. Your blood, your soul," Drake says as he steps closer to him with a screwdriver in his hand. I stand back, my arms crossed over my chest, and watch the man work.

To say he was disturbed would be an understatement. The things he's doing to Malley are disgusting and sinister. I have no problem torturing a man, but this is something else.

George's screams pierce my ears as I stand back and watch the man do what he does. The girl from the van seems to be interested as well. She hasn't left or even looked away, but after the hell she was forced to endure, why would she?

"Anyone want a turn?" Drake asks over his shoulder as he pulls Malley's tongue out of his mouth and holds it with a pair of pliers. He has a pair of some sort of scissors in the other hand. I shake my head, happy enough to let him do his thing here.

"No one?" he asks once more when the girl moves. She walks over and takes the scissors from his hand before finishing cutting off his tongue. Blood squirts around the room as I take a step back to avoid the spray. She doesn't, though. Instead, she stands right there next to Drake and watches.

"Damn, sweetheart. Didn't think you had it in you," Drake tells her.

"I have a lot of hate in me." With that, she turns and walks out of the shed before slamming the door closed.

"I need to stick around for this?" I ask Tyrant.

"No, why?"

"I'd rather be with the girls that watchin' him do his thing," I admit.

"Go. We got this. Just let them know it's over, yeah?"

I nod my head. "I can do that." I turn on my heel, taking one last look at the asshole who orchestrated all this and head out of the shed. I'm halfway to the clubhouse when I see Bell coming my way.

"There's a girl covered in blood," she says.

"Not hers. Come on," I tell her just as screams rip through the night.

"What's happening back there?"

"You don't wanna know, darlin'. Just go back inside."

"What's happening?" she asks, looking up at me with those big beautiful eyes.

"It's over. That's what's happening. Everything is ending, darlin'. We got the motherfucker who started this. We got his ass."

"Are they-" She can't finish that sentence.

"Yeah, they are. He won't be alive much longer."

"I don't know what to say."

"Say you love me, Bell. Tell me you love me."

"I love you, Ryan." I lean down and kiss her roughly, taking what belongs to me. I take it all because she's mine. She's everything I could have ever wanted and more. I take what she's giving me and then some.

"I wanna hold you all night tonight. Fuck the rest of this. I just need to know you're mine."

"I am yours. Don't you think we should tell Ruby?"

"That we're currently torturin' a man in the shed?" I chuckle as I shake my head. "I don't think so."

"She needs to know this is over too, Ryan. She needs that closure."

"We'll let Shade give her that."

"You think those two really care about each other?" she asks me. I honestly don't know. Shade doesn't really get into his feelings.

"I think she needed someone, and he was there. I think he'll still be there, but I don't know how far that relationship will go. Shade isn't like me. He doesn't care about people easily. It's hard for him."

"What about you?" she asks.

"What about me?" I wrap my arm around her shoulder as we walk back toward the clubhouse together.

"You care, don't you?"

"I told you I loved you. That means I care, Bell. I'm not ever lettin' you go. You might as well get used to the shit that goes on around here."

"What if you change your mind later?" she asks softly. Is that what's bothering her? I pull my arm free, step in front of her, and grab her face in my hands before kissing her hard.

"I'm not goin' anywhere, and I'm not changin' my mind. You're it for me, Bell. You're everything I've ever wanted."